D0597177

The Vacant Casualty

PATTY O'FURNITURE

The Vacant Casualty

BOXTREE

First published 2012 by Boxtree
an imprint of Pan Macmillan, a division of Macmillan Publishers Limited
Pan Macmillan, 20 New Wharf Road, London N1 9RR
Basingstoke and Oxford
Associated companies throughout the world
www.panmacmillan.com

ISBN 978-0-7522-6543-8

1 3 5 7 9 8 6 4 2

A CIP catalogue record for this book is available from
the British Library.

Printed and bound by CPI Group (UK) Ltd, Croydon, CR0 4YY

Visit **www.panmacmillan.com** to read more about all our books
and to buy them. You will also find features, author interviews and
news of any author events, and you can sign up for e-newsletters
so that you're always first to hear about our new releases.

The Vacant Casualty

Prologue

Mrs Elizabeth Bottlescum always pottered around the garden in the very first moments of the day. Primarily this was because she always woke so early, but it was also due to the little gossipy titbits she could glean while she watered the azaleas.

For there was much gossip to pick up in the small town of Mumford. On the surface it might appear a sunlit vision of English perfection, a sleepy idyll of old-fashioned good taste and family values, but if one knew where to look it was packed to the rafters with rotters of the first water.

It had been many years since Mr Bottlescum passed away, and left her alone in this little house. She often thought of him now, not because he had been particularly interesting, or because he had any even mildly pleasant personality traits, but because he'd been in possession of an absolutely colossal wanger. On warm summer evenings, she often daydreamed about it for hours.

The beauty of this setting could not be denied. The early sun rose slowly in the East over the hilltops, glowing pale orange. In the narrow streets, the cottages with their thatched roofs and whitewashed walls slumbered in silence. Ducks fretted playfully in the millpond, while a gentle morning wind drifted with dandelion seeds. And from the freshly tilled fields that surrounded the town at not a quarter of a mile's distance drifted the aroma of twenty thousand tonnes of cow shit that had been spread there the previous afternoon. It was the country. What can you do?

In just over an hour the local little darlings would be threading their way happily down the hill towards Pigfarts, the exclusive local school – and at the sight of them Mrs Bottlescum would wonder for the hundredth time why they always carried broomsticks and had what looked like gunpowder stains on their uniforms. The pips signalled the end of *Farming Today* on Radio 4 and the beginning of the morning in earnest.

The blessing of being awake at this time was in the comfort to be taken from the various routines that one could always observe so early. First, one saw Mildred Penstroke's dog, Glands, taking a colossal dump on the neighbours' lawn, as she had painstakingly trained it to do. Then came Hetty McBride sneaking back from Bill Strange's house, where she had spent the night, and pretending not to notice Mrs Bottlescum's bald gaze. A minute later Hetty's husband, Lionel, came out of the next-door-but-one house and scurried ashamedly in through his own back door.

'So it begins. Do you know what, Pocket?' she said to her cat, which purred quietly by her ankles, 'I think it's getting warm enough for us to crack out the old deckchair, you know . . .'

And so she toddled off to the shed and shortly returned, set out the aforementioned apparatus and sat back in it with a deep sense of pleasant relaxation and a quiet thrill at the entertainment to come.

Moments later, Mrs Glendinning from number 47 peeped round the door of the Smythington abode before making a dash back to her own house, shortly followed by three other women, who all dispersed in different directions.

'Lesbo tryst,' muttered Mrs Bottlescum, returning from the kitchen with her breakfast on a tray.

Next it was Reggie Farmhurst and Oliver Patchbury who snuck out of the disused windmill, no doubt woken from their carnal slumbers by the crowing of the cock.

'Gayers,' said Bottlescum, munching a bit of toast. 'They tie each other up in there, you know, Pocket.'

She finished off her tea as she saw the entire local fire department abseil via their hose from the bedroom window of one of the town's more notorious teenage girls – followed shortly afterwards by the first fifteen of the Mumford rugby league team.

'Good Lord, how does she fit them all in that tiny

bedroom?' Elizabeth wondered. It brought to mind an incident from her own childhood in a similar rural village, when she had celebrated St Swithin's Day 1944 by entertaining a dozen members of the Airborne 353rd Regiment of the United States Air Force. 'The young do have to try and take things *further* these days,' she tutted. 'Perhaps young Penelope could hold one of her soirées in a Mini Cooper – invite a brass band along to play "Abide with Me" and we can get someone from *Guinness World Records* along. Hah!'

The morning's amusement was nearly at an end. Almost everyone in the town was now safely returned to their own beds. There were only a few last stragglers remaining – the local piano teacher sidling from the pet shop wearing a nasty smirk and some mysterious stains on his waistcoat, and someone in a nun's costume leaving the Catholic church. But then, she supposed, it was possible that it was actually a nun.

'Stranger things have happened, Pocket!' she said, and her cat assented with a mew.

At last, with nothing remaining of her breakfast but an empty cup and saucer, and some breadcrumbs scattered down her blouse, she was about to pack up her things and go upstairs to wake up the major and tell him to get back to his wife when she spotted something that was, for once, out of the ordinary.

Down the lane that led out of town was tripping that man from the Parish Council. The nice one, what was his name? – Terry Fairbreath. He was known thereabouts as just about the only person who could be relied on to give an issue a fair hearing, the rest of the council being filled with ancient madmen, cranks and troublemakers. He was handsome too, and considered quite the catch by the local females (even the group Mrs Bottlescum had referred to under the appellation 'lesbo tryst' had considered making him the first male member of their little gathering), yet he always remained single, was always composed, thoughtful, polite and well turned out. It was a mystery to everyone.

'Well, not *that* much of a mystery. Gay as a peacock, no doubt. But then the gayers had no luck with him either . . .'

After re-entering the house she washed and put away her breakfast things, and it was only on the stairs that it occurred to her there was something strange about his appearance. It was not simply the fact that he was out so early, although that in itself was unusual. Perhaps it was that he had been carrying an axe.

Was that it, she pondered, or was there something else as well?

Yes, surely it was that he had been dripping blood from a conspicuously large wound in his back. But there was something else . . .

Was it that he had been carrying a smoking shotgun

under one arm? Well, he had, but that wasn't what was niggling at the back of her mind. Was it that glimpse she had caught of someone leaning out from the bushes, pointing a bow and arrow at him? Perhaps. But there was another detail that lingered there, waiting to be found.

Maybe it was that his coat flapped open and she had caught sight of what looked like a fat pack of dynamite strapped to his chest, with a jolly modern-looking digital countdown, and a string of hand grenades.

'Yes, that was it,' she nodded to herself. 'It was that, and the fact that he was sprinting fast as he could go, screaming, crying and begging for his life. That was definitely what caught my attention . . .'

She pondered this strange circumstance for a moment before shaking her head. It was all too much for a sex-mad septuagenarian like herself to take in.

'Ah well, I'm sure there's a perfectly innocent explanation,' she said quietly, hoisting herself up the few final steps before entering her room and slapping the major's backside with all her might.

And yet, when the town's citizens rose (again) from their beds later that morning and went about their business, they would find that not only had Terry Fairbreath gone missing, but that his disappearance was just the beginning of the terrible sequence of events that would result in catastrophe.

Chapter One

THE POLICE STATION in Fraxbridge received the call at eleven o'clock on the Monday two weeks following. Mr Fairbreath's cleaner, Mavis Ritter, had gone as usual to let herself into his home and discovered the front door wide open. Feeling somewhat concerned, she decided she ought to check with Mr Fairbreath that there was nothing amiss and so, once she had taken her customary four shots of gin from his 'secret' bottle in the airing cupboard and (after whipping her duster quickly across the top of the microwave) put in a couple of hours at The Elder Scrolls V: Skyrim on his Xbox 360, she took the five-minute walk round the corner to the architect's office where he worked. On enquiring after his whereabouts, she discovered that he had not been into work for ten days, and was not answering his mobile phone. She decided to put the matter in the hands of the police.

Mumford itself had the smallest possible police station a village could have, a cubicle adjoined to the Town Hall not much larger than an old-fashioned police phone box. In fact, this is exactly what it had been until the town's sole part-time community officer, PC Staplethorpe (in whose person was also made up the body of Mumford's traffic police and its Territorial Army), converted it into a small kiosk in which he could sleep off his hangovers under the protection of the law, and away from his wife, Angela. The station was, therefore, so unused to receiving allegations of serious crime that when he got Mavis's report, Staplethorpe had no choice but to give it pride of place in the centre of the orange plastic 'My First Business desk' children's accessory, which was all that could be fitted into the office space underneath his hammock.

This was Staplethorpe's personal technique, which had until now proved 100 per cent effective. All crimes in Mumford came face to face with the complete indifference of the law, and eventually turned out not to be crimes at all (cats returned home, surreptitiously borrowed items were replaced in the dead of night), or were retaliated against in a petty enough way to teach the perpetrator a lesson.

Thus Mavis's report of the missing Terry Fairbreath remained under the scrutiny of the law (in the shape of PC Staplethorpe's backside as it swung to and fro) until two weeks had passed, when, having achieved no results from the local force, Mavis deemed it advisable to put a call through to the police station in Fraxbridge, the next town across.

Mumford, as I have attempted to convey, was a sleepy little town hardly worthy of the name – a swollen village, really, of perfect Englishness. It had a millpond; it had a cricket team; it had an ancient abbey that required millions of pounds for its upkeep, for no visible benefit; it had quaint thatched buildings, winding streets, curious little shops and hundreds of white-haired denizens who tended their gardens, waved happily to one another in the street and considered their lives to be blessed.

Fraxbridge, by contrast, but five miles away, was considered by the upstanding citizens of Mumford to be a plague-ridden city of vice and corruption. It had, after all, a railway station, by which undesirables could come and go as they pleased. It boasted also a chain bookshop ('The one that begins with W', Mumfordians would tell you darkly, disdaining to actually say the word), and a *Marks & Spencer*. All these things placed the town beneath contempt and of course contributed to its need for a substantially larger police force.

Thus it was that when Mavis Ritter telephoned Fraxbridge Police HQ in some considerable distress two weeks after her original report, the missing persons case found its way onto the desk of Detective Inspector Reginald Bradley. It arrived just as he received a call to tell him he had a visitor in Reception.

'This isn't ideal timing,' he thought to himself, reading

the report and starting to feel anxious. Bradley had never had a missing persons report. He had never had a report of any kind at all. The truth is Bradley had until this point spent his entire seventeen-year career policing in a small village twenty miles south of there, and had only the shadiest notion (gained from watching half an episode of *NYPD Blue* when he was fourteen years old, which he had switched off out of fright) of what 'real policemen' were like. The only exemplar to have crossed his path so far was the hard-bitten cop who occupied the desk next to his, Detective Brautigan, a physically huge man, hard-packed with loathing and frustration, who could regularly be seen punching the inside of his windscreen as the sports results were read out over the radio, and who sometimes chewed whole packets of cigarettes rather than walking seven paces to smoke outside on the fire escape.

Bradley was not sure he could live up to this, this life of a cop in the 'big city', as he considered Fraxbridge to be, with its two betting shops, its amusement arcade and its Wetherspoon pub. In fact, shortly before he received the written report of a missing person named Terry Fairbreath and the telephone call telling him his expected visitor (one Mr Sam Easton) was waiting in Reception, he was wondering whether there was a chance that, after being promoted so suddenly a week before, he might be able to avoid ever getting any cases at all.

'Perhaps if I take up smoking, I could always dart out for a cigarette whenever the phone rings,' he had wondered, just as the phone had rung, and he had, without thinking, answered it.

'Sam Easton in Reception for you,' said the voice.

Too late.

He rose from his desk and marched to the stairs, thinking that at least a missing person case would give him something to talk to his visitor about. As he went down into Reception he spruced himself up in the reflection of one of the windows, and ran a hand over his hair, smoothing it onto his head.

He reached the reception area, somewhat anxiously distracted, and as he spotted his visitor, a slim youth in a hoody top, he waved. Unfortunately at that moment Detective Brautigan came into Reception ahead of him. Like a furious bull fixing on a feeble matador, or some smaller creature it considers a natural enemy, he made a compressed grunting noise and charged over.

'Detective Inspector Bradley?' asked the young man, in a rather worried voice.

Brautigan, already travelling at thirty miles an hour, reared somewhat.

'Bugger off, shithead!'

The youth thought about this for a moment and clearly

decided it was some sort of joke, so he gave a high-pitched laugh.

There were probably many things you could do in front of the astonishingly muscular Detective Brautigan to escape an immediately violent response. Setting off a nuclear weapon, for instance, might be one possibility. Escaping down a wormhole into another dimension in space and time could be another. Laughing, however, was not one. The large man picked the youth up, spun him round and bounced his face off the window five or six times before saying into his bleeding ear:

'Listen up, gobshite. My colleague Bradley here's got a writer from London coming in to talk to him later. The last thing he needs is a fucking teenage reprobate getting under his shoes and taking the piss, OKAY?'

Having smashed the youth's face against the glass a few more times, he noticed that this had left a rather unpleasant smeary mark, so he deemed it advisable to wipe the face up and down to try and buff the glass, and teach the lad a further lesson.

It was as he was judging that he had done a fair clean-up job that some other more urgent thought popped into Brautigan's head. He dropped the youth, darted out of the room, climbed the stairs and disappeared from sight.

Bradley felt somewhat awkward as he made his way over to the young writer, helped him to his feet, dabbed some of the blood from his nose, introduced himself and invited him to come upstairs for a sit down.

The young man had not yet had the chance to recover fully, and simply nodded. As they walked, Bradley made an attempt to make light of the other detective's behaviour.

'That was an example of exactly the sort of thing which we *don't* approve of here in the Fraxbridge police community. But my colleague has been investigating a number of murders in the local area, and I'm sure you understand, at times of stress, tempers run high. I don't think he could imagine someone as young as you being a writer. Here you go, sit down,' he said, before adding simperingly, 'May I fetch you a coffee?'

The youth nodded, looking dazed.

'Latte? Espresso?' enquired Bradley, almost falling over himself.

The other cleared his throat and said a cappuccino would be great, and Bradley left him at his desk while he went to fill a cup with the foetid ash-grey froth that spewed from the hissing machine in the corridor.

'Is *that* a cappuccino?' asked the writer dubiously, looking down at the cup he was handed.

'It came from the machine after I pressed the cappuccino button,' said Bradley, before conceding, 'but that is far from the same thing. I certainly don't advise drinking it –

the rats don't touch that stuff. You'd probably get botulism or dengue fever or something.'

The writer nodded somewhat mournfully and contented himself with sniffing the drink instead, discovering that Bradley was in fact right. The revolting smell made him snap his head back up, which sudden movement at least had a ghost of the revivifying effect that a bolt of caffeine would have done.

'Again, I am most *dreadfully* sorry for my colleague's earlier behaviour,' said Bradley, leaning over the table. 'It was most uncharacteristic.'

The writer shook his head to rid himself of the shock.

'Not at all,' he said. 'In fact, that was exactly the sort of behaviour I was hoping to come across.'

Bradley looked confused.

'You see, I'm here to study cops. I'm just a lily-livered writer from the leafy suburbs but I want to get to know the real workings of the police force inside out. I'm working on a novel – a gritty crime novel that I hope to make into a series of novels. And then, perhaps, one day, a really great, hard-hitting TV series.'

'I see,' said Bradley, whose eye wavered from the young man to the report on his desk, his mind rapidly trying to calculate which of these to pursue first for the least disappointing outcome. He did not feel confident of either.

'To have experienced police brutality at first hand –

well, it will be very useful as a . . . a sense memory, if you will, when I'm writing. I'm Sam Easton.' He offered his hand.

The detective took it, looking as relieved as he was grateful, and drawing his chair in closer to his desk, he leant across once more and said confidentially: 'You see, I don't want to disappoint you, but I'm not really that sort of policeman at all. I was only made a detective last week. I'm just trying to live up to expectations.'

'Right,' said Sam dubiously. 'Whose expectations, exactly?'

Not even daring to point directly towards his fellow officer, Bradley indicated over his shoulder and Sam followed his gaze. There at the next desk sat that other detective, who had appeared to Sam no more than a terrifying blur. Now he had a chance to take him in. He was a bruising hulk of a man, bald and with sweat patches sprouting from beneath his arms. There was a Chinese food carton on one side of his desk, along with a half-eaten burger the size of a sponge cake. As Sam looked on, he gargled a hefty measure of brandy like mouthwash, and splashed the remains of the half-bottle into his coffee cup.

'Detective Brautigan,' Bradley whispered. 'He's a *real* policeman.'

'Maybe I should be following him around, then?' suggested Sam hopefully.

'You wouldn't survive a week,' said Bradley. 'None of his partners ever do.'

'God DAMN IT!' screamed Brautigan from the next desk, making them both jump. They looked around to find that he was talking into his telephone and staring down, eyes bulging, at a square open box that had just been delivered to his desk, his expression a mixture of fury and revulsion. When his voice at last broke forth, it sounded like a Formula One car coming out of a tunnel at full pelt.

'I said JAM doughnuts! NOT RING DOUGHNUTS! Get it right next time or I'll punch your fucking nose out through your arse!' He smashed the receiver back into place so hard it snapped in half and, snarling, he pulled the line from the wall and tossed the whole pile of junk into a corner, where it landed on a heap of discarded telephones. Then he turned to the little old lady sat primly in the chair next to his desk and pointed at her with a finger trembling with fury.

'You sure it's a Pekingese you lost? God damn it, give me the *truth*!'

The lady nodded mutely.

'You better not be fuckin' lying to me,' he screamed, his voice becoming hoarse. 'Okay, tell me – where did you last see the little motherfucker?'

'Or, actually, maybe I would be better off with you after all,' Sam conceded quietly.

'Indeed,' said Bradley. 'Come on, let's get out of here. The eleven o'clock snack trolley's coming round and he always flips out when that happens. I've got a missing person report to investigate and there's only so much of him I can take.'

'NO FUCKING CREAM BUNS!'

Brautigan's voice followed them down the corridor as they left.

Chapter Two

THE CAR JOURNEY to the little town of Mumford, just five miles over the hill, was spent in thankful silence. When they arrived they found a conurbation so small it consisted of scarcely more than a square with a large medieval coaching inn and a modest Town Hall at opposite ends, with two main roads running off it, and a small number of streets spreading away, boasting a smattering of twee-looking shops.

They found Terry Fairbreath's house down one of these quiet lanes, and waiting for them outside was Miss Mavis Ritter. She explained the situation in a good deal of distress and then showed the two men through the house. From the first moment the detective had no apparent compunction in including Sam in every step of the inquiry – whether out of hope for his assistance or sheer lack of the necessary presence of mind to ask him to remain outside, the young man could not tell.

As Mavis had predicted, the house showed no signs of disturbance, and in fact after investigation of the missing man's effects, all of which seemed to be in perfect order, they still had no evidence at all to show why he should have absconded so suddenly and completely from his life.

Standing outside and thanking Miss Ritter once again for her assistance, Bradley asked if she knew who else of Terry's acquaintance they might interview. She sneezed twice, as was her habit when being asked a question to which she did not immediately know the answer, and after elaborately mopping her face, said doubtfully that she did not know his friends, but that they might speak to the members of the Parish Council, of which he was a member.

In fact, she said, looking at her watch (and sneezing once more), she understood that there was a Parish Council meeting going on this moment, at the rectory.

The men were not much sooner informed of this than they were knocking at the rectory door.

'What do you think?' said Bradley as they waited to be let in.

'About what?' Sam asked.

'About the Parish Council,' said Bradley. 'Do you think it might throw up some hints?'

At being asked this, Sam started to have serious misgivings about placing himself with Bradley. For research into a novel about bumbling inadequacy, he was beginning to think, the detective might be the perfect subject. But for a brutal cop drama that dealt with real problems, he was coming over a little like a wet fish. As a young man who had grown up reading books and dreaming of being a writer, however, Sam knew a great deal about acting like a wet fish, and he felt a pang of sympathy. For his own selfish purposes, he wanted the detective to have a difficult case to crack, which he could be in on, but for this rather plain and simple man's own self-esteem he wanted it too. He began to think about fictional detectives he knew, from whom he could glean some useful lessons to toughen up Bradley's technique.

'I'd say this might prove useful,' he said. 'You never know what matters get discussed in places like this.'

The bell was presently answered by the vicar's lady help, a hunchbacked woman who showed no sign of human intelligence, but who merely blinked and led them along a dusty corridor towards a room at the back.

'Go on,' whispered Bradley.

'Well, you never know,' said Sam. 'In a little place such as this, the Parish Council can be a hotbed of secret motivations and simmering resentments that are generations old. The sort of thing that could lead to murder . . .'

'Next on the agenda,' a man's voice intoned gravely from within the room as the door opened before them, 'something that has caused deep division among us . . .'

Sam and Bradley exchanged a meaningful look as they

passed into the room and made their way towards some spare chairs at the back.

'. . . the use of Rich Tea biscuits with our refreshments. I refer to Mrs Bloodpudding's request for a change to Custard Creams.'

The detective and the writer both looked rather depressed as a murmur of discord went around the room.

'Bloody outrage,' muttered a deranged-looking old man with a copper complexion and wearing half-moon glasses over an eyepatch. 'We've been eating Rich Teas since 1964. Thin end of the wedge. It's like Nazi Germany!' and he smashed the table with his fist.

No one paid any attention, and the second the old man realized this, he seemed to calm down completely and began munching away quite happily on the Custard Creams that were being handed round. The new biscuits met with a widely favourable reception. A vote was briefly counted and agreed upon before they moved on.

'Next,' said the chairman, a handsome, expensively dressed middle-aged fellow with an easy manner, 'the problem of how we should treat the tourists who visit and are seeking the, er . . .' Here the man, who showed every sign of being a confident public speaker, suddenly stumbled on his words. 'I notice we have visitors . . .' he mumbled.

'I don't get it,' barked the old duffer at his elbow. 'What's the problem with tourists, Selvington?'

'Ah, this must be Lord Selvington. Owns half the country hereabouts,' whispered Bradley into Sam's ear.

'Please, Major, some decorum,' begged Lord Selvington. But the major looked like someone who possessed the magic trinity of bad hearing, an enjoyment of making a nuisance of himself and a dislike of decorum.

'Don't see the problem with tourists, Selvington,' he said. 'We *rely* on tourists. That's why all our bloody shops are called Ye Olde Shoppe, even Ye Olde DVD Shoppe. I mean, it's bloody ridiculous.'

The other members of the council were now noticeably agitated at the major's interruption, and were trying to shush him, while several others looked over their shoulders at Sam and Bradley, who remained mystified.

'Ye Olde Hatte Shoppe,' the major went on. 'Ye Olde Booke Shoppe. Ye Olde Cakee Shoppe, that's a bloody joke . . .' At last the old man caught on that people were trying to quiet him. 'Oh, I see!' he said. 'When you say tourists, you're talking about people who're looking for that famous woman who moved onto the h—'

Here he was broken off by a shushing that suddenly jumped in volume until several people in the room were actually shouting — one artistic-looking man jumped from his chair and sang 'LALALALALA' at the top of his voice, then when everything was under control threw himself back into his seat and hummed tunefully as though it had all been part of the song that was playing in his head. The major was quietened, and a very uneasy silence descended on the room.

Sam looked left and right, awkwardly, and scanned for an exit closer than the door he had come in through. He wondered if they had wicker men in this part of the world. He looked at Bradley, who was sitting back in his chair, with one leg over the other, his foot swinging happily as though nothing had happened.

'I don't know what the major refers to,' said Lord Selvington stiffly. 'But to put it baldly, yes, there are lots of misguided tourists in the town who are looking for the private home of a very famous author. Of course, we know this is nonsense . . .'

As he said this, he could not help but cast a quick and meaningful glance towards the tall window to his left. Neither could the rest of the council – their eyes travelled as one to the view of the crest of the hill, topped by a tasteful detached house in pale stone, surrounded on each side by stands of trees, silhouetted by the bright afternoon sky and framed perfectly by the bay window. Their eyes all lingered on this charming scene for a moment too long, before drifting distractedly back to the business at hand.

'. . . Er . . . Nonsense . . .' said Lord Selvington. 'As I said. There is absolutely no world-famous author of a series of fantasy novels that have been turned into major motion pictures, trying to live her private life (to which she is perfectly entitled) anywhere near here. And I'd say that to anyone. Er, please,' he said, mopping his brow nervously, 'what's next on the agenda?'

A lady on the other side of the table, the only member of the council unmoved by the distraction owing to her furious concentration on the minutes, peered down through her glasses and said:

'Point three. Application by author Stephenie Meyer to build a huge mansion on the top of the hill.'

'Oh, bloody hell,' said Selvington. 'Not another one. No, no!'

The others seemed to join in with this sentiment, and the matter was quickly voted down.

'Next,' said the severe-looking lady with glasses. Then she blinked, and refused to read the minute out loud, passing it instead along the line to Lord Selvington.

'Ah,' said the peer awkwardly. 'Bad news from the golf club.'

'Oh God,' said a round little man a few places along. 'Not the Oldest Member again?'

('I think this guy's the mayor, the little chap,' whispered Sam to Bradley.)

'Is it the same trouble as last time?' asked the mayor.

'I dunno, what the fuck happened last time?' chimed in the major, looking towards Selvington.

'Oh, *please!*' expostulated two of the ladies (who sat beside one another, dressed identically, and appeared to be twins), speaking at once.

'It's funny, isn't it,' whispered Sam into Bradley's ear, 'that the words "mayor" and "major" are so linguistically linked?'

'Hmm,' said Bradley.

'I suppose etymologically they probably mean the same thing,' Sam pressed, feeling he deserved a little more than this. 'Interesting, don't you think?'

'Hmm,' said Bradley.

'I don't suppose you mind if I stick my hand up my bum-hole and then smear it over your face?'

'Hmm,' said Bradley. '*What?*'

'What *has* he been up to at the golf club?' demanded the major, adjusting his eyepatch.

'Well, he's been getting his, er . . . well, his *member* out again. In the bar, apparently.'

'Oh Lord! There wasn't a party of Japanese schoolgirls being shown around like last time, I hope?'

'Apparently no. It seems this time he was genuinely worried that he had something wrong with him and was trying to get attention.'

'Well, of course he was trying to get attention, it's the oldest trick in the book.'

'Yes, but ironically it didn't work. Everyone just pretended not to notice for two weeks . . .'

'*Two weeks*?' interjected the detective.

'Well, yes,' said the mayor, addressing the visitor directly. 'They are rather used to this sort of thing, I'm afraid. And of course he was rendered speechless by pipe smoke and whisky, back in the nineties . . .'

'Which was when he was only in his eighties . . .' muttered the major.

'So in a way he was the old boy who didn't cry wolf. Apparently he was horribly infected – they got him into the operating room and lopped the thing off, and luckily there were still signs of life after the operation.'

'In what, him or the penis?'

'Moving on . . .' said Lord Selvington. 'If I could take us beyond scurrilous gossip, we have genuine issues to get to on these minutes, as we are all aware. Can we get through the frivolous stuff so that we finish before *The Archers* comes on this evening?'

Sam smiled to himself at this remark, but was startled out of it by Bradley whispering urgently into his ear: 'Oh God, we're not likely to actually miss *The Archers*, are we?'

'I think it's unlikely,' he whispered back. 'I think he was being hyperbolic.'

The detective was clearly panicked by this mysterious word, and, wanting to indicate that he knew what it meant, he grasped hold of the most vulgar misapprehension, jumped up in his seat and uttered, 'How rude!' loud enough to attract disapproving tuts from half a dozen councillors.

'I just meant he was being a bit over the top,' whispered Sam, trying hard to keep his temper, and therefore the volume of his voice, under control. 'If you miss it, you can listen to the repeat tomorrow at two o'clock, for heaven's sake. Or on Sunday. Or on bloody iPlayer. I won't spoil the plot for you, I promise.' Oh Christ, he thought. What the crapping hell am I doing here?

'Minute seven: the employment of split infinitives in the council minutes,' said the chairman. 'Now this really is a problem . . .'

At this moment Sam, who had been alternately swearing and blaspheming under his breath for several minutes, began to wonder quite seriously what his life was coming to. As a freelance writer he was not only unaccustomed to being stuck in a school-assembly situation like this where he was not allowed to move, or speak, or light a cigarette, but he was also comparatively unused to being up at two in the afternoon. And so – contemplating that if he got into a filthy mood at the beginning of a meeting which might very well last longer than *Lawrence of Arabia* then he would be in a terrible state by the end of it – he attempted to calm himself down with a cool appraisal of the members of the council.

This was aided by a sheet of paper being thrust into his hand by a friendly lady councillor, who had taken pity on the newcomers and passed them a set of minutes each.

Now, he thought, looking down the list. Who is who?

'I'm *hungry*,' whispered Bradley into his ear, with the spontaneous impatience of a child. 'Do you think we're allowed biscuits?'

'For Christ's sake!' Sam said aloud, discovering after the fact (as happened to him too often) that he had involuntarily lost the temper he had been struggling to control. He strode across the room and stole a plate of biscuits from in front of one of the men before returning and plonking it on Bradley's knee. This produced the sudden and unexpected reaction of someone beetling across to serve them both with a cup of tea – this person being the stark and expressionless old crone who had earlier let them in.

The basic English cup of tea, Sam reflected as he took a grateful sip, was the one hot drink which was not drastically impaired by being made on a massive scale.

Bradley picked up one of the biscuits and said, 'Oh, Custard Creams. Wizard!'

At once everyone in the room swivelled their heads to look at him.

'She DOESN'T LIVE HERE!' bellowed Lord Selvington. 'Get it? Now, no more talk of wizards!'

This startling outburst compelled Sam and the detective

into silent obedience as the cups of tea were handed to them, and the meeting slowly resumed.

SETTING HIS TEA down again, he muttered into Bradley's ear: 'This town had better have a fried chicken joint and a kebab shop or I'm going to have a conniption.' Let him deal with that, he thought, as he picked up his copy of the minutes. Now, who were all these dusty old freaks?

First name: 'Major Simon Ernald Stuyvesant Eldred, MC'. Okay, that one's easy.

Second: 'Eric Barnes (Mayor)'. Also easy: the short, fat bloke who didn't believe anyone was looking at him, and was picking his nose. Then there was name three: 'Lord Selvington of Butterhall (Jimmy)'. Yes, despite Sam's inherent dislike of people who owned more than a dozen (or quite possibly, several thousand) times more money than he would ever earn in his life, this guy looked the sort of posho who was sane enough to have the nickname Jimmy. As opposed to, say, Boffles, or Twiddlesticks, or something.

Next, four and five: 'Miss E. Quimple and Miss M. Quimple'. Easy again – the two identical ancient old bags on the right of the table, both staring into space.

Six: this one startled him. 'Saracene Galaxista, High Church of the Milky Way'. I didn't notice anyone who looked like Ming the Merciless's sister when I came in. But wait – this one was not hard to spot. There she was, clear as day: a dyed-in-the-wool hippy with wild grey hair and a severe expression, wearing a waistcoat decorated with the animals of the zodiac in gilt.

The next few were just as straightforward.

Seven: 'Rt Revd. Archibald Smallcreak, Rector'. Almost certainly the bored-looking sixty-year-old thin bloke with an androgynous expression.

'It was him,' thought Sam. 'It was him, with the lead pipe, in the milking parlour. I bet he's an old perv.'

Eight: 'Miss G. Elvesdon, parish librarian'. The thin, slightly younger (i.e. under fifty) lady in the corner.

Nine: 'Mrs Bloodpudding'. Surely the sweet-smiling, permed octogenarian by the major's side.

Name number ten: 'Walerian Exosius'. What the *hell*? Who would be called – oh, but wait. There he was, too. A lanky fellow, almost collapsed over his own chair in a pretence of exhaustion. Violet neckerchief wrapped thrice around his throat. High cheekbones. Hint of vulnerable disdain, as though he had just smelt a disgusting scent he was unsure was not his own. Sniffing like he has a cold, and looking around to see if anyone notices. He must be an artist.

Although there were still a few of the full roster to identify, Sam was distracted out of his reverie as he realized the split infinitive debate was still going on. While he was paying attention to the grammatical argument, D.I. Bradley got up and handed a short note to Lord Selvington, who read it, then looked up and nodded importantly at the policeman.

'Uhum,' Sam coughed politely as he interjected. 'There's, er . . . nothing wrong . . .'

One by one the councillors ceased their yelling, or earnest talking, and turned to him. He cleared his throat once more before saying, 'I apologize for speaking uninvited, but there's actually nothing wrong with using a split infinitive. Linguistically. Grammatically. There never was. Avoiding it is like using "serviette" as a posh replacement for "napkin", when the Queen herself would use a napkin. A false nicety. *Fowler's Modern English Usage* has said so for over eighty years; Kingsley Amis agrees. And many others. In case you were interested.'

'And you are . . .' asked one.

'A writer,' he said, and choosing not to meet their eyes, he sank back into the darkness, but secretly hoped they noticed his hoody. After consulting his iPhone in the shaded security of his lap for a few moments he looked up to find Bradley leaning over him with a leer.

'You *are* a ponce,' he whispered.

'At least now we can proceed with the important matter at hand (thank Christ),' said Lord Selvington, 'which, as we all know, is that our good friend and fellow councillor Terry Fairbreath went missing last week. Here I ought to introduce Detective Inspector Bradley, who will be leading the investigation.'

'Oh good Lord, has he been *murdered*?' uttered one of the Miss Quimples.

'No, no——' said Bradley, putting up his hands. 'Really . . .'

'Dead, you say?' barked the insane major from the other side of the room. 'Damn shame! Hope it wasn't poison.'

'Oh great Scott, I hope he hasn't been murdered,' said the other Miss Quimple. 'He made a smashing *Tarte au Citron*.'

'And he owed me seventy quid,' said Walerian Exosius. Then he laughed nervously. 'But that's hardly a reason to murder someone.' And he giggled even more nervously, before turning dead serious, twisting his head on one side and adding: 'Unlike fucking my sister.'

'For *God's* sake, calm down!' shouted Sam, once more discovering he'd lost his temper shortly after it happened, but also, an instant later, pleasantly surprised by the results. All heads turned to him, and then to the inspector.

'This is a missing persons case,' said Bradley. 'There are countless reasons for a person to be missing that are incredibly simple. Misunderstanding, bad communication, forgetfulness, sickness . . .'

'Having your brains blown out . . .' added the major.

'Having your brains blown out,' repeated the inspector, to gasps from around the table, before adding, 'is only one of a million possible reasons. So I wish you would do me a favour and help me do my job. Which is to say, please make yourselves available to have a chat with me as soon as you can – in the next twenty-four hours, if possible. Please leave your names and addresses with my assistant.'

'This total ass has got an *assistant*?' wondered Sam for a moment, before realizing that the detective was talking about him. His mouth began to form the words, 'You can go and f—' but then he grasped that, just like being briefly beaten up and having his face smacked against the window many hours earlier, acting as a detective's assistant during an investigation could be invaluable experience in helping him write a future police drama.

TWENTY MINUTES later, walking to the car, they compared notes. Bradley read over the minutes and Sam held a smoking cigarette in one hand while he rolled a second cigarette in the other.

'Not the hotbed of suspicion that I entirely predicted,' said Sam regretfully.

'Well, no,' admitted Bradley.

'Do you think he's still alive?' asked the writer.

'I've no idea. It seems there are lots of strong characters in this place, at the very least. So lots of things to examine before we really know . . . where we are . . .' Bradley turned away and looked frowning into the distance. Sam followed his gaze. There didn't seem to be anything of particular interest in the distance.

'Are you, er . . . Are you trying to look mysterious?'

Bradley squinted sideways at him.

'Sort of. Is it working?'

'No. No, not at all. I think the rules are that you can do that towards the end of a case, when there are lots of things to ponder and all the clues are up in the air, and you're waiting for the hairs to rise on the back of your neck.'

'The back of the neck?' asked Bradley, feeling with his hand inside his collar, and appearing to brush upwards to make them stand on end. 'Why do they do that?'

'Don't force it, Bradders. I think it's got to happen naturally or not at all. Here, let's get in, it's cold.'

Sam climbed in and put on his seatbelt while the detective seemed to wrestle with the handle to his own car. This guy, he reflected, was not perhaps Inspector Morse material, but he was also rather sweet. Already Sam could feel himself see-sawing between feeling exasperated and wanting to wind the guy up, and feeling fond of him and wanting to give him advice. This was probably going to be a wasted research trip, he was realizing – but seeing as he was supposed to be down there for a week, he might as well enjoy himself. He thought about that for a second, considered his own nature, and knew if it was to be achieved, he was definitely going to have to wind this guy up. As far as he would go. In fact, he decided, he would try to turn him into a *real* detective, by which he meant, a *fictional* detective, as Bradley seemed to wish to be. He had time to enjoy these thoughts at leisure as the detective inspector climbed inside, got his wrist caught in his seatbelt and then elbowed the horn lengthily while trying to extract himself, which drew the attention of a dozen or so local folk.

'Hey, Detective,' said Sam. 'By the way – what's your first name?'

Bradley noticeably hesitated and said tentatively, '. . . Reginald.'

'Reginald's fine. What's wrong with Reginald? Lots of upstanding people have been called Reginald. But your first name isn't Reginald to me any more, okay?'

'What is it, then?'

'It's "Detective". How does that make you feel?'

Detective Inspector Bradley shrugged, but failed to conceal that it did give him a small burst of satisfaction to be so addressed.

'Okay then, Detective, that's settled. And one other thing: if you let me, I'll buy you a pint later and we can discuss the case. Who's our first witness?'

'I thought we'd start with the man in charge – Lord Whatsisname. We should have spoken to him after the meeting but he seems to have gone home. Apparently he lives three miles away.'

'Okay, do you need me to navigate?'

'Not really. We can see the house from here.'

'Where? Behind that castle?'

'No, I think that *is* it.'

'Oh, yes. Right. God, that really is a big pile, isn't it?'

'You can't smoke that in here, sorry.'

Sam flicked one cigarette out of the window and tucked the other behind his ear while Bradley pulled away, and began to negotiate the twists and turns of one of the town's half-dozen roads.

As they passed through the square, Bradley concentrating with needless intensity on his driving, Sam caught sight of a curious situation. In the middle of the square were parked over a dozen mobility scooters, each of them with a granny sitting on it. But his first instinct, which was to think what a sweet sight it made, was quickly eradicated by a second glance. The scooters were parked in perfect formation, making an arrow shape. There were perhaps fifteen of them. And the old ladies were not primly sat on the seats, looking straight ahead as he had come to expect. Some of them were seated with one leg cocked over the side, others had got out and lolled against them, and appeared to be rolling cigarettes. As he watched, one of them made a remark, her face wearing a mean expression, and the others laughed along with her sneeringly. It only lasted a moment, but as the car swept across their vision, Sam could have sworn that three or four of them turned and tried to stare him out. One of them spat some chewing gum onto the floor and wiped the dribble from her mouth without her eyes leaving him.

Then they were driving swiftly down a side street, and the strange sight was gone.

IN LESS THAN ten minutes they were turning in at the gate along a mile-long drive lined with plane trees, and as they pulled up outside the vast mansion a few minutes later, an open-top sports car screeched past, spitting gravel and braking only about eighteen inches short of crashing through the enormous oak front door.

'Sorry about that,' said the young man who climbed out, extending his hand. 'I just hate a needlessly long walk, what? Still getting the hang of this thing. I'm, ah . . . You know, what?'

'We're here to see Lord Selvington,' said Bradley, clearly awed to be in the presence of genuine aristocracy.

'Oh, the old man. He's bound to be knocking around the place somewhere.' Having escorted the two gentlemen inside, he shook hands with them both once more. 'The name's Horace. Hey, come through to the old thingy what-sit room here, we'll have a cocktail.'

He burst energetically through a pair of tall doors and they found themselves in a modest room no wider and taller than the average aircraft hangar, across which the young aristocrat bounded with energy towards a table bearing a drinks tray on the other side. The other two looked around themselves. There were divans and sofas dotted about, and vast portraits of disapproving males on the wall.

'Does he appear a bit eccentric to you?' asked Bradley.

'I think he might have been drinking,' said Sam.

'What makes you say that?'

Sam cleared his throat. 'Well,' he reflected, 'the first we saw of him he nearly killed himself with the most violent piece of drink-driving I've ever seen. Then he forgot his own name. He had an open bottle of martini *in his hand* when he got out of the car, and . . . he now appears to have just fallen fast asleep on the carpet.'

'Good Lord, so he does.'

Leaving him where he lay, the two men went looking around the house for someone else to speak to, and they came across Lord Selvington in his library. After some momentary surprise at finding them standing there, he invited them back into the drawing room for refreshments and they were relieved to find that in the meantime Horace had come round and sat himself down on a sofa.

'Lord Selvington . . .' Bradley began.

'Jimmy, please.'

'I'm not called Jimmy,' said Bradley, his face blank. 'Oh,

I see, *you're* Jimmy. Well, er, Lord Selvingtonjimmy, we wanted to ask you what you know about Terry Fairbreath.'

'Of course,' said Jimmy. 'Well, what can I say? He was liked by everyone. Friendly, approachable . . .'

'You weren't aware of any problems in his life?'

'None at all. He was very successful.'

'And you weren't conscious of his having made any enemies?'

'No. But you must understand – he had the deciding vote in the Parish Council, and there are lots of important issues on which his opinion would have a big effect on people's lives.'

'Such as?'

'Well, Mumford is a quaint old English town, and that inevitably attracts various money-making schemes but we are very careful to keep the place true to its own nature and not give in to commercialism.'

'I understand. There seems to be an implied "but" at the end of that sentence . . .'

'Yes. Of course not everyone in the town is exactly rolling in money, so each time we quash one of these schemes, in essence lots of them lose substantial income.'

'Schemes such as what?'

'A plan to build a massive hypermarket just outside town. That would have brought a lot of investment. There are film crews here constantly too, and we have to pick and choose which ones we allow.'

'Film crews!' said Bradley. 'How interesting. What sort of thing?'

'Well, just this year we've had *Songs of Praise*, *Time Team* and *Antiques Roadshow*. Had to say no to that Bill Oddie chap.'

'He's an arse,' said Horace, coming round from another swoon and looking slightly haggard. It appeared his hangover was setting in.

'And there was supposed to be a *Vicar of Dibley* movie shooting, but we said no to that as well.'

'Really?' asked Sam. 'Seems a little late, doesn't it?'

'They were doing a zombie mash-up, apparently. Calling it *Vampire of Dibley*, or *I Spit on Your Nave*, or something. I forget.'

'So there's more to this place than meets the eye,' said Bradley, rather pointlessly. Sam stared at him for a moment and decided he might as well wade in himself – and why not be bad cop?

'What were you doing two weeks ago today, when Fairbreath was last seen?' he said.

'In Scotland, hunting deer with Prince Philip.'

'Oh *yeah*?'

'Yes. I was.'

'I see. Well, thanks very much.' He couldn't think of

anything to come back to that with. He'd have to work on his routine.

'Well, you've been very helpful,' said Bradley. 'And may I ask you on a personal note, why did you make that very specific point about a world-famous author of a series of supernatural-themed children's books *not* living here?'

Behind him, Sam slapped his forehead in disbelief.

'Ah, I see,' said Lord Selvington. 'Ahahaha. Yes, indeed. Well, you see, she *doesn't* live here. Definitely not. And I can add to that, as her neighbour – rather, as I would be if she *did* live here, which she doesn't – I've *never* been round for dinner, and she *doesn't* make an absolutely smashing beef stroganoff. You see? Eh? Hahaha!'

'Right,' said Bradley, looking so utterly confused that he might actually cry. 'Well, as I say, you've been very helpful. Who do you recommend we talk to next?'

'If you're going to talk to everyone anyway, I suppose you could go to Major Eldred next. He's quite insane but at least that will be more amusing than discussing literally any-thing with the Miss Quimples.' He wrote down the address on a page from his diary, and tore it out. 'Here you go.'

'Thanks,' Bradley said, as they got up.

'Nice to meet you,' Sam told Horace, the only person he had warmed to so far, who was following them towards the door. 'Tell me, Horace, what's your proper title?'

'Hmm?' the young aristocrat remarked. 'Oh, I, er, what is it? Sir Egbert de Montfort Herringbone Lambsley.'

'So Horace isn't your real name at all?'

'Oh yes, it is. Don't let's get into this, it's frightfully complicated. Look, do you want to buy some bennies?'

Although Sam had been offered drugs many times before, he had never been asked this specific question (and certainly not in such plush surroundings) so it took a moment for him to catch on. Then he saw a whole week in this sleepy place stretching ahead of him, and was decidedly tempted. But they had now emerged into the sunshine and the detective was waiting by the car door only ten paces away, so he felt he must refuse.

'Shame,' said Horace abstractly, looking up at the clouds. 'Maybe I'll go and play with some Lego . . .'

Sam bade him goodbye and was driven away, wondering all the way whether he had been joking or not.

Chapter Three

BRADLEY AND SAM parked near the Elk & Catalepsy pub, neatly tucked away off the main street, and briefly discussed going in. A line of schoolchildren filed past, chatting and laughing. For some reason, the left arm of every single child seemed to be invisible, but no one in the busy street appeared to notice anything strange in that fact. Sam blinked and turned again to Bradley, motioning towards the pub.

'Come on,' he said. 'It's gone five o'clock. Drinky drinky time.'

'I can't drink, because then I can't drive home,' said the detective.

'Come *oooooon*,' said Sam. 'What is it, a ten-quid taxi ride back to Fraxbridge? I'll give you a tenner, and claim it back from tax.' Bradley at least had the presence of mind to frown disapprovingly for a second or so while these words sank in.

Seventy seconds later they were receiving their first pints over the bar, and less than two minutes after that they were sitting at a table on the street outside the pub. Sam lit a cigarette, inhaled deeply, blew a smoke ring and puffed the rest out in a contented sigh. Bradley, following his lead, took a deep sip of his beer, then looked blinking up at the sky and sighed, his shoulders falling.

On the street either side of them were ancient cottages, perhaps two or three hundred years old, many with thatched roofs. They were buckled and twisted with age, and from their gardens and window boxes shone explosions of bright flowers, lilac, orange, white and pink. Although it was only early evening the street was completely empty, and a warm breeze blew gently down it. The light chattering rhythm of birdsong was in the air and altogether the scene presented a picture of perfect seclusion and contentment.

'What do you think of the place, Mr Easton?' asked the detective, his senses clearly overcome by the setting. 'Quaint, is it not?'

'Yes, it's quaint as all fuck,' the writer said. 'It makes me want to kill myself.'

'Yes, yes, quite,' said Bradley, without the smile leaving his lips. 'Funny what he kept saying about that famous female fantasy writer who doesn't live here, wasn't it?'

Sam sighed. 'Yes,' he said, sloshing the beer around in his glass tiredly. 'It's a complete mystery. Whoever can he have meant?'

'Diana Wynne Jones?' mused the detective. 'No, I believe she passed away. Ursula K. Le Guin, then, perhaps? Ah well. This *is* a lovely little town though. I should dearly like to live here – me and Mrs Constable both. Sorry, Mrs *Detective*, I should say. But it's too pricey for us, I fear.'

Sam was three quarters of the way through his pint, feeling the first gently enjoyable shine of tipsiness. He was already trying to calculate whether he could get away with nipping inside for 'another round' and managing to down a secret extra pint and whisky chaser before coming back out with the next beers without arousing suspicion. But the detective's words made him stop for a moment, and consider the man he was talking to.

'So you've only just been promoted?' he asked.

'That's right,' said Bradley.

'But you must have been trying for it for ages? I mean, that's a big step.'

'Big doesn't cover it. I was only a regular plod two weeks ago.'

'But hang on, hang on! This must be some sort of a big deal for you. You are at least pleased?'

Bradley looked awkward. 'If I'm honest, it was my wife's idea that I go for promotion. I was amazed that I got it.'

'Why? You've worked for years, decades even, to get to this point?'

'That's true,' Bradley conceded. 'I mean, I plodded away happily as a country bobby.'

'And you're a clever fellow with an eye for what's going on,' lied Sam.

'That's true as well, I hope,' said Bradley, brightening somewhat.

'So now you've got the job, what's the problem?'

'I'm not one hundred per cent convinced I was the right guy for it,' conceded the other man.

Here, Sam disappeared into the pub on the pretext he had planned, but once inside decided not to keep his fellow drinker waiting while he downed an extra pint, instead returning with a tray bearing two pints and six shots of sambuca.

'Explain,' he said, setting down the tray.

'I'm not really a detective inspector at heart,' admitted Bradley.

'Oh come, come, you can't get to do that job without being good at it, I'm sure.'

'Well, you see, they were going to promote Wickfield to CID, but he died suddenly of a heart attack.'

'Right. So what? You couldn't have been far behind this git Wickfield in their esteem – or rather, *Wankfield*, as I call him.'

'Easy. He was my best man.'

'Okay, sorry, go on.'

'And then Georgy Tallbone got himself into some bother with a complete fuss over nothing – something the papers called "human trafficking". He had to resign. It was PC gone mad.'

'Quite literally, by the sound of it,' said Sam. He gestured to the shots on the tray.

'And Detective Constable Hanover's resigned to have a sex change.'

'Do you mean he's resigned to having a sex change, or he resigned in order to— oh, never mind. Here you are, anyway. And you're on this case. To you!'

'That's right,' said Bradley, downing the first of the sambucas.

'And I'm sure you're going to solve it!'

'That's RIGHT!' said Bradley, raising the second of the sambucas to toast it. 'Tell me,' he added, his speech already alarmingly slurred. 'What was it that you wanted from this assignment?'

Sam was at this moment reflecting that his mild-mannered companion was well on the way towards being fully plastered, while he himself was barely making the first pleasurable inroads into mild drunkenness. As a cautionary measure, before he could answer the question he downed the remaining sambuca shots, and in order to keep up with the detective, asked for six more from a passing waitress.

'What did I want from a detective?' Sam asked. 'What

did I *really* want? Well, I don't know, maybe things like . . . Okay, here's a shopping list. One: sudden, brilliant and unpredictable leaps of logic.'

Bradley coughed, and something revolting slipped out of his nose. He busied himself about getting rid of it with his handkerchief.

'Two: a chase of some sort. A high-speed car chase, preferably, and which ends with some sort of death-defying crash. Like going right through a shop's plate-glass window.'

Bradley nodded intently, pocketed his handkerchief and in doing so knocked over his drink.

'Oh, for pity's sake. Miss!' barked Sam at the waitress, who didn't seem to have moved since he had spoken to her. 'I distinctly asked for six more sambucas.'

'I think that's actually a poster with a picture of a waitress on it,' said Bradley, looking up from where he was mopping the beer with a copy of the *Daily Mail*. 'And she seems to be dressed in the style of *fin-de-siècle* Paris.'

'*What*? Is she? Oh, yes. Maybe I don't need them after all.'

'And third thing on your shopping list?'

'Third, a terrifying game of cat-and-mouse with all of our lives at stake, possibly ending with the killer being blown away with a high-velocity assault rifle.'

Silence descended on the little table beneath the hanging basket of dahlias.

'I'm not sure you've got a very realistic picture of police work in this part of the countryside,' Bradley said apologetically.

'Maybe not,' said Sam, resting his face on an upturned palm and looking around the pretty square gloomily.

'What is it that you write, then?' asked the detective, with the natural weariness of one who anticipates having to feign interest.

'Ah, well . . . You wouldn't have heard of it. It's just rubbish, really . . .'

'No, go on,' said Bradley despite himself. 'I'm interested.'

'Well, I've not written any crime novels *yet*,' admitted Sam. 'That's why I'm here now, to do the research. What I've done up to now has been quite different.'

'So what sort of thing . . .'

'You know those silly humorous books that get sold by the till in the run-up to Christmas?'

'Oh, yes,' said Bradley. 'I got that one about commas. Or was it apostrophes? I got four copies of that.'

'Yes, well, things like that.'

'But not actually that.'

'Well, no. By the time I was getting involved it was all about parodies to do with animals. You know, silly made-up facts about nature. *Do Bears Crap in the Woods?* was one of mine.'

'Oh,' said Bradley. 'Good for you.'

'Well, it sold a few copies.'

'And do they?'

'What? Oh. No, they go in fully automated bear-toilets these days. Or if they do, they have to scoop it up, you know,' said Sam. He kept an eye on the detective to see whether this response was taken seriously, but he couldn't tell.

'Right,' said the detective. 'So that's what you do.'

'And ghostwriting. *Andy McNab's Middle Eastern Cookbook* was one of mine. And Lord Sugar's second memoir, *One Lump or Two*. The first draft, anyway, before I got fired. Predictably. But I've had enough of all that. I want to break out into fiction, so I'm going to write a police thriller.'

'I have to admit I would have thought a sleepy countryside detective story was right out of fashion. I'm surprised you think this sort of place would be good to set a thriller in.'

'What, here in Snoresville-upon-Yawnington? God, no. I mean, I want the thing to sell! A hot crime novel these days is about police corruption, terrorism and serial killers. If you want to get a six-figure, multi-book deal, it's got to be written so any TV series adaptation would run for five seasons at least. Mine's set on the council estates of Hackney.'

'But that's where you live, isn't it?'

'Yes, that's right.'

'Well why didn't you do your research on your own doorstep?'

'All the East End cops are already hired as consultants by ITV, you see, so I had to look further afield.'

'But surely there's someone closer . . .'

'Elephant and Castle have signed a deal with several movie production companies, the rest of south London are Channel 4's beat, and by the time I found a police force who didn't have an exclusivity contract with someone or other I was out here in the countryside.'

'Right,' said Bradley. 'Well, I hope I can be some help, at least.'

'Of course you can! Don't want to sound ungrateful for you giving me your time – I've stumbled right into the heart of a mystery, so I'm happy as Larry.'

'Right. And who's Larry?'

'I think we need more sambucas.'

Chapter Four

SAM HAD A vague memory of making a reservation at a cheap and cheerful-sounding bed and breakfast just outside Fraxbridge, but as he woke up he realized he had no memory at all of checking in. He felt a soft cushioning sensation beneath his head before a sharp and antagonistic pain began to fizz behind his eyes. This was a familiar feeling – a pain that was not simply just there, throbbing away, but which danced along the nervous system as though blessed with demonic intelligence, intuitively switching all the time to wherever he expected and most wanted it not to be.

Resigning himself to this familiar horror, he sat up, and discovered three very unwelcome things: that the sun was up, that he was in someone's front garden and that he was wearing a car tyre around his waist like a tutu.

'Oh dear,' he said, as is customary on such occasions. He inwardly considered trying to wriggle out of the tyre before standing up but, concluding that this would be more painful and complicated, was relieved when he got to his feet and the rubber ornament slipped to the ground of its own accord. 'Perhaps I wasn't actually *wearing* it at all,' he thought, 'Maybe I fell asleep in the middle of a hula-hoop experiment.'

At that moment, he caught sight of the early-morning procession of children towards school. He woozily leaned on a fence post and tried to remain inconspicuous as they passed, but couldn't help finding something curious about the sight. Perhaps it was the fact that they wore old-fashioned long cloaks over their uniforms, or that as they laughed and joked, they pointed little sticks at each other in a curious way, as though they were wands, and chanted funny phrases, and showers of sparks or plumes of purple flame leapt out at them. Perhaps it was because one of the children, getting into a fight with one of the others, was suddenly attended by a giant dragon wreathed in green smoke that attacked his adversary – or perhaps, Sam wondered, it was that the group of teachers who ran to catch up with the pupils and castigate them all resembled well-known British character actors – he could have sworn he made out Dame Maggie Smith, Timothy Spall and Miriam Margolyes, and he thought he could see a Helena Bonham Carter in there as well. But almost as soon as it came into view, the procession had passed, and Sam was left wondering whether he was simply drunkenly hallucinating.

He had, after all, some more immediate problems to contend with. He did not particularly want to chance the potential rusty squeak of the cast-iron gate, due to the risk both of detection and acute head pain. Instead, placing his feet with care between the beautifully spaced flowers and holding back the wild plumage of the plants in front of him, at last he clambered over the low wall onto the street, and there, temporarily feeling rather pleased with himself (owing to the remaining alcohol that was still swimming through his system), he began a search for the detective.

It was not a very long or difficult task. Despite the apparent quaintness of the Elk & Catalepsy pub, Sam's last memory was of plucking filled shot glasses from the between the landlady's voluminous breasts. He had a vague sense that there might have been a karaoke night going on at the time, and that he had seen someone riding the detective around like a donkey, before sticking a carrot up his bum. But then perhaps that had been just a dream.

Sam thought he also remembered finishing the contents of the last seven glasses on the nearby tables and then briefly losing consciousness, then coming round, and rushing the stage before being kicked firmly out of the venue by the owner only moments ahead of the be-wigged, be-lip-sticked, be-boa-ed and be-high-heeled inspector. Indeed, even as Sam recalled them both stumbling out of the door opposite where he stood now, he caught sight of the detective fast asleep, sitting up in next door's carp pond.

'Come on, old chap,' he said, heaving Bradley up and

helping him, dripping, along the road. 'Let's get some breakfast.'

'No matter what you do to me, I will survive,' murmured the detective in his ear.

'No doubt about that, old bean – but then that depends if you can survive breakfast at Mrs Bagley's cafe.'

He tumbled the sleeping figure into the seat opposite him at an outside table as a pretty waitress came out to greet them.

'Do you have a "wake up" breakfast on your menu?' he asked.

She smiled brightly. 'Yes, we do.'

'Could you get that for him – does it include a bucket of water in the face?'

'I'd love to help you,' apologized the girl, looking at the comatose policeman, 'but I'd have to mop it up myself. And that's not going to happen.'

'I need to wake him up somehow. If I give you two quid, will you kick him in the nuts for me?'

The pretty girl pretended not to hear, smiled even more brightly, then blinked and tapped her notepad impatiently with her pen.

'Okay,' said Sam. 'We both want coffee, orange juice, pints of tap water, and I'd like lots of bacon and eggs and beans and toast. And Tabasco sauce. Or hot pepper sauce, if you have it.'

'We do,' she said, smiling.

'Brilliant,' said Sam. 'By the way, how's my flirting? It's terrible, isn't it?'

'Yes, it's rotten,' she smiled and escaped inside.

'Again,' he muttered, grinding his teeth. 'Why must I act like this always? I meet an angel in human clothing and I gibber like Hannibal Lec— Oh, hello.'

'Hello,' said Bradley from the opposite chair. 'Am I . . . alive?'

'Yes.' Sam saw a small light of hope come into Bradley's eyes just then, and he knew the thought process behind it well: 'If I am not dead, then perhaps I will soon die, and this won't hurt so much?' He leant over and grabbed the other's arm to assure him he was firmly in the corporeal world.

'Tough shit, boyo,' he said. 'We're in this together. Didn't you say – or sing – "I Will Survive"?'

'Oh, Christ,' said the other man, lowering his face to the table. 'My head . . . my . . . my head . . .' He then looked up to the sky briefly before closing his eyes again. 'And my bum!'

'This is it, man,' said Sam happily. 'You're a real cop. You're hungover to hell. Look at you!'

'Really?' asked Bradley, looking up through bloodshot eyes. 'This is what it takes?' He seemed momentarily cheered by the prospect.

'Well, not *entirely*. What it really takes is a number of

deeply ingrained issues which you are emotionally unable ever to conquer, a far-right-wing world view and deep, deep loneliness. The loneliness that only a certain hooker with a heart of gold can quench.'

Bradley gratefully took the coffee that was handed to him by the waitress, and stared through his hungover gloom at Sam.

'This,' said Sam, 'this is pretty much the lot of the proper detective.'

'Feels like shit,' said Bradley, with uncharacteristic candour.

'That's because it *is*. But imagine the way the day goes from here. First, coffee . . .' Sam pointed, and Bradley sipped.

'Oh God, that tastes good.'

'First food tastes better – *unbelievable*. The salt rush from the bacon, the crunch of the toast, the soft egg . . . Then you're in fighting mode.'

'Fighting mode?'

'Come on, Reginald, you're a *real dick*.'

What pride the detective had gathered itself into a somewhat awkward haughtiness. 'Well *you're* not so much yourself!' he said.

'No, man, I didn't mean dick. I meant a *dick*. As in, detective.'

'Oh, yes.' Bradley gulped down a mouthful of hot

coffee, hiding the intense pain it caused his lips, tongue, mouth and throat to do so.

'So . . .' said Bradley. 'Oh Christ . . .'

Into Sam's chest at that moment entered a feeling as close to being fatherly as there could possibly be between a twenty-something middle-class boy and a man at least ten years his senior. He poured Bradley some more water from the jug that had been placed between them, put sugar in the other man's coffee and stirred it in, then proffered the cup and asked for more orange juice.

'You'll be okay,' he told him soothingly. 'It's just a hangover. You'll be fine by lunch.'

'I'll be *dead*,' said Bradley.

'Here are your breakfasts,' announced the waitress cheerfully, setting down plates laid out like faces, with eggs for eyes and curled sausages making smiley mouths. With his fork Sam turned each of the sausages the other way round, so they were less mocking. Little if anything was spoken for the next ten minutes, save for single-syllable grunt-like requests for sauce or condiment, and gasps of appreciation and relief.

At the next table the artist they had seen at the meeting yesterday, Walerian Exosius, was looking even more mournfully hungover than they were. Sam watched wearily as he devoured his vegetarian breakfast, then staggered to the curb, threw it up into the gutter and began to weep uncontrollably.

At this sight Sam moved his plate away, unable to face any more, and drank his cooling coffee as if it were life-giving serum.

'So you say you've read lots of detective novels?' asked Bradley, when he could speak again.

'Yes . . .'

'And seen lots of police dramas?'

'Lots. Why?'

'You'll keep on giving me tips, won't you?'

'Of course I will, you lunatic, Detective Bradley, but I'm supposed to be asking *you* for tips, you know. That's why I've come down here!'

'Well, yes, I know,' said Bradley, looking abashed. 'But the reason *I'm* here is really to do with Mrs Detective. She loves the idea of being married to a detective.'

'And you want to learn from the guys off TV?'

'The boys in the office don't seem to respect someone coming from out in the sticks like me. I mean, *further* out in the sticks. They haven't given me much other guidance . . .'

'Okay,' said Sam, rubbing his hands. 'Then I have lots of advice to give you.'

'Like what?'

'Well, you've got to be a hard-boiled motherfucker,' said

Sam. 'Yes, two more coffees, please,' he found himself saying a moment later as he saw the waitress was hovering.

'Hard-boiled,' said Bradley. 'What does that mean?'

'It means you don't take no for an answer from nobody.'

'You mean I *do* take no for an answer from *somebody*?'

'*No.* I mean not even from me. You're a proper detective, you're headstrong. You don't give a fuck what no motherfucker thinks.'

'Right,' said Bradley, nodding with concentration as though someone had just explained a specifically difficult method of parking. Behind them both, Walerian Exosius had taken out his camera and was photographing his ex-breakfast, while still weeping.

'You don't *care*,' said Sam.

'Right,' nodded Bradley.

'If I argued with you right now you'd have a fit and handcuff me to the table, even though we're friends. That's how tough you are,' said Sam.

'Right,' said Bradley, closing a metal cuff over Sam's wrist and linking it into the arm of his chair before he could protest. 'I'm going to the loo.'

Sam swallowed several violent compound expletives as he watched his companion rise and go inside.

'I can't even reach my iPhone with my spare hand,' he muttered. 'This would make a great tweet.' He leant forward to see if he could pluck it from his top pocket with his teeth just as the waitress arrived again.

Raising his startled face to see hers as she took the plates, Sam realized that for once in his life he had the chance to give the impression of being a dangerous young man (locked as he was to the furniture). Trying to make this impression while having a brain that felt like it was filled with cotton wool and shattered glass, he succeeded only in simpering pleasantly while she picked up the plates, refusing to meet his eye or acknowledge his existence but, as she turned away, giving the artist a cheery little wave.

'See you tomorrow, love!' she said.

'Cheerio,' said Walerian, wandering off, mopping his tears with his neckerchief.

'Where have you been?' Sam whispered viciously as Bradley sat back down. 'I've been humiliated in front of that deliriously beautiful waitress, you *pig*! Did you see her hair? It *cascades*!'

The detective unlocked the handcuffs with slow clumsiness.

'Okay,' said Sam, rubbing his wrist, 'I have to admit that was an excellent first step. You have to take that attitude into literally every walk of life. You don't take no for an answer from nobody. But let's make me the exception . . .'

With one of his freed hands he took a pepper cruet and stuffed it up Bradley's nose.

'What-AHHH-ah-ah-AAAH-AHCHOO! I'm sorry about that, Sam – ahCHOO! I wasn't sure I'd have the courage to try it out on anyone else.'

'If you want to get more advice along those lines, I'm the one you're protecting, you understand? I'm Al Capone. Or . . . Well, the protected one, whoever that would be. Come on, let's walk. Wash that!'

His last words were addressed to the waitress, who had reappeared from within the cafe and to whom he handed the pepper cruet wrapped in a tissue.

'We'll be *back*!' he added, pointing at her in what he realized was a not very charming and possibly somewhat threatening way. 'Okay, style it out,' he said to himself, turning back round and brushing down his jacket and tie.

They were only halfway up the street towards the small car park where Bradley's police carpool vehicle was parked, but the detective now put a hand on his arm.

'I can't drive it,' he said.

'Oh, come on, Cinderella,' said Sam, before he felt the tremor in Bradley's arm. Then he saw the man was standing stock still. He recognized what was going on, and he knew what to do.

First, he sat the detective on a low, thick stone wall from which he would find it nearly impossible to fall. He spoke to him as loudly and clearly as to a child trapped in a lift.

'THIS IS THE FIRST MAJOR SYMPTOM OF YOUR

HANGOVER KICKING IN,' he said. 'THEY ARE REALLY
RATHER UNPLE— Wait a minute, I can't keep shouting
like this, I'll give myself an aneurism.' He sat down next to
the detective instead and held his hand.

'You see, you have much too much alcohol in your
bloodstream. Now you've eaten, you're starting to metabo-
lize some of it, and it feels like a real bastard.'

The detective nodded stupidly, as though his body was a
clumsy suit worn by some smaller intelligent creature
within.

'You're lucky, I know what you need,' said Sam, looking
encouragingly into his eyes.

'You're the reason I *need* it,' whispered Bradley vaguely.

'Come on, Goldilocks,' said Sam, 'I'm just trying to
make you a real detective. Just stay here and I'll be back.'
With that he let go of Bradley's arm and vanished round the
corner, for all the detective knew, to catch a bus to
Heathrow, or fetch a camera. But sooner than he expected
here was the young lad back again, with a white plastic bag
full of encouraging bulges.

'Eating that breakfast helped you *begin* to get lots of stuff
out of your system,' said Sam. 'There are a lot of things you
don't understand about the hangover.'

'I've been hungover,' protested Bradley.

'In 1996,' said Sam. 'Things have come on. Look here.'
He held up the bag. 'At least this place has a working

pharmacy and newsagent.' He performed each of these operations twice: taking out a bottle of spring water, opening it, taking a long sip and then tipping in a couple of Alka-Seltzers. Then cracking open a second can of fizzy orange-flavoured drink and setting it on the wall alongside the first before opening another bottle of water and mixing in a diarrhoea cure, which (he had been told) contained many of the essential body salts that are sacrificed by a night's drinking.

Sat on the wall, the two men doggedly drank through all three containers until they were empty. They sighed, and gulped and gawped; they stretched, liquids fizzed in their stomachs and various facts of the world seemed a bit more realistic and manageable. Bradley tried to work out whether he could dry his clothes and where, or when he might get other clothes while these ones dried.

'Why did you let me sleep in that fishpond?' he asked.

'I don't remember having much of a choice,' said Sam. 'The last I remember you were kissing me and telling me that I really have to follow my dream, that I really, really have to follow it. Then I sang "Suzie Q" by Creedence Clearwater Revival and we got chucked out. That *was* a karaoke night, wasn't it? Not just someone else's table we invaded?'

'Okay, that's enough,' Bradley said. 'What was that we were drinking, by the way?'

'Sambuca, for the most part.'

'Well, it's revolting. I can practically taste it in my ears. Is there a dry-cleaning place in this town?'

'Dry-cleaning places don't actually *dry* your clothes for you,' said Sam, sitting heavily back down on the stone wall. 'Oh, crap, you know what? Your hangover is about to lift and mine's about to start. Come on then, Tinker Bell, where are we going next?'

Chapter Five

SAM AND DETECTIVE Inspector Bradley visited the two Miss Quimples next. It so happened that the Miss Quimples were twins, and as we have seen they were both on the Parish Council, where they sat alongside each other, dressed identically. It didn't come as a huge surprise, therefore, to discover that Miss Emily Quimple and Miss Cecily Quimple lived beside each other in perfect picture-box cottages on the south-facing upper slopes of Church Lane, which was marginally the poshest of the town's nine streets.

The two men approached the left-hand cottage and after knocking on the door were received by a little old woman wearing a cream blouse and black skirt, who regarded them with a shrewd eye.

'Come about Terry, have you?' said Miss Emily Quimple, and walked through to the living room, allowing them to follow her. 'I'm afraid I've very little to offer you.'

Sam was just thinking that if he saw any food he was likely to chuck up, when he discovered that this wasn't true. He saw what she meant by 'very little' when the little old lady brought through a plate with an iced gingerbread on it, followed soon after by another tray containing a large pot of tea.

'I'm sure I'm just a silly old biddy,' she said. 'But you were here to ask about that fellow Terry Fairbreath, who went missing?'

'That's right,' said Bradley. 'What can you tell us about him?'

'Well, he was a prostitute,' said Emily Quimple. 'Is that the word I mean?'

The two men looked at each other.

'I doubt it,' said Sam.

'I'm sorry, who are you?'

'Me? I'm a writer.'

'Oh, a writer,' said Emily, welcoming one of her cats onto her lap. 'So not a policeman, then.'

'No,' said Sam.

'So you don't really have a reason to speak at all?' she asked, with a friendly smile.

'None,' admitted Sam, taking a slice of gingerbread and turning to Bradley. 'Your witness!'

'Can you think of anyone who had a grudge against Terry Fairbreath?' asked the detective.

'Yes,' said the old lady in a considered tone, looking up at the coving. 'Anyone would. He had . . .' she thought about the phrase for a long time before looking them both in the eye, one after the other: '. . . no morals.'

'You mean because he's gay?'

'He's *what*?' she said, and Bradley could see he had soured her day all the way through, simply by mention of the word. By his side, Sam (who was enjoying an excellent slice of gingerbread) wondered for a moment if she was going to deny knowing what the phrase even meant.

'Well, we don't know that for sure,' said Bradley, rapidly trying to recover his composure. 'I was just asking if you thought he might have been. He led a secret life . . .'

'It's mere conjecture,' said Sam. 'Writers use it too, to explore how people will react to questions.'

'He was a friendly young man,' said the old woman, making herself appear friendly by a visible force of will. 'But he had strange ideas.'

'Such as?' asked Bradley.

'Go on, Bradley,' Sam was thinking. 'Keep asking, man. This cake is delicious. Don't let me ever stop eating this cake . . .'

'He brought in lots of new concepts to this village that we would rather have kept outside.'

'Like broadband?' asked Sam, chewing.

'Yes, exactly. We're old, and we don't like having to deal with new words on a weekly basis. *Broad*band! What does it mean?'

Sam made a shallow nod that he hoped expressed that she had uttered a profound rhetorical question, and took another bite of cake.

'And rimming,' she went on.

At this, Sam's oesophagus went through a sequence of sudden violent oscillations, and a small piece of gingerbread wedged itself firmly in the middle of it.

'Rimming, dogging, barebacking. We don't like these things,' she said equably to Bradley, as Sam coughed so violently into his napkin he felt his vocal cords might snap. 'We're an *old-fashioned* village, you see.'

'Rimming, dogging,' noted Bradley, quite innocently, as Sam began to cough blood. 'Sounds like a load of hyperbolics to me. And I understand he moved the flower show from June to August.'

'Exactly.'

'Scandalous,' said Sam, just about squeezing out the word while clutching his throat.

'We think so. The flower show has been in June since I was a little girl.'

'And that must be . . .' said Bradley, before allowing his thoughts for once to go a little ahead of his mouth, and trailing off.

'Go on, Detective,' said Sam, before washing down his ravaged throat with a full cup of tea, and then throwing three more pieces of moist gingerbread (with its delicious crème fraîche icing) onto his plate.

'Well, some time ago, I suppose,' the detective said. 'By "we", do you mean you and your sister?'

The little woman's features sharpened. 'No,' she whispered. 'No. "We" means the council. Not her. Not . . . the *other* one.'

Bradley looked bemusedly over at Sam, who was doing his best to appear thoughtful while trying to make his mouth large enough to admit two squares of gingerbread at once. 'I always thought that identical twins had a special . . .'

'No!' shrieked the little woman, looking at Bradley without noticing her outburst made Sam choke on an even larger slab of cake. With her spare hand she unconsciously plucked two knitting needles from a ball of yarn and stabbed them deep into the upholstery with a squeaking sound. Then, at the thought of her sister, some awful emotion overcame her. The men exchanged a glance, wondering whether what they were about to uncover might have anything to do with Terry Fairbreath's disappearance.

'You see,' said Emily, 'my sister is a *terribly vicious bitch*!' And she kicked the air with one of her sharp little feet. Sam's eyes bulged stupidly and he made gasping noises as Emily tottered to the window.

'Look,' she said. 'It started with the objects being thrown over the fence – a dead cat, a rusty wheelbarrow,

the Mayor of Oxley. Then she paid ruffians from the slaughterhouse to scatter animal entrails all over the garden.'

'Ruffians?' asked Bradley.

'Slaughterhouse?' croaked Sam.

'*Entrails!*' whispered Emily. 'The shitguts!'

Sam threw himself over the back of his chair and
coughed a chunk of cake across the room into the glowing
fireplace, where it landed with a sizzling splat. 'How
absolutely offal,' he said, looking unduly pleased with
himself for a second as he straightened up, rubbing his
diaphragm before falling back, wheezing, onto the seat.
'Offal, eh?' he repeated, looking around, disappointed with
the reaction.

'Hmm,' he thought. 'I think I may still be drunk from
last night.'

'*Look*,' said Emily.

'Oh,' said Sam, joining her at the front window.

'She tries to ruin everything I do.'

In the carefully tended garden outside, which was
divided up into neat squares and oblongs devoted to
separate fruits and vegetables, a number of plants had
been gouged out of the earth in an aggressive fashion,
then smashed up. The whole production might have been
intended at first to indicate that it was the handiwork of
an animal, but it seemed the person responsible had en-
joyed themselves too much, for shoe prints were clearly

visible in the mushy remains of a particularly large and fleshy marrow.

Looking Emily up and down and judging that she wouldn't see seventy again, Sam suddenly pictured a bitter history of sibling hatred that spread back to the second Churchill government at least. He surmised that her sister's vindictive act could not be the first, and almost certainly there had been retaliations. 'You take this sort of thing lying down?' he asked.

'Christ, no!' declared the old lady. 'I had a male rattle-snake imported from New Mexico last spring and let it go in her house but she got lucky and trod on its head with her stiletto. *Slut!*'

'So your vegetables are important to you?' asked Bradley. 'You enter them in competitions?'

Emily simply looked at him.

'That's a yes,' said Sam in his ear. The writer, ever intrepid and eager for danger, was already chewing another slice of ginger cake. 'Local flower show, you know.'

'I'm not averse to a bit of gardening myself, Mrs Q, I don't mind telling you,' said the detective. 'I've had some melons in my time . . .'

This was, however, but a hollow distraction from the sight now unfolding in front of them, for a truck was unloading what looked like ten or twenty tonnes of compost directly onto Emily's garden. Both men stared open-mouthed, but as the oozing brown liquid cascaded down and squeezed among the trellises and pots and nets, the old lady was no longer watching. She had turned away and tapped a speed dial on her phone.

'Terence,' she said sharply, 'we have a code red. That's right – the eagle must raid the nest. I REPEAT,' she repeated, 'THE EAGLE MUST RAID THE NEST! We have go!'

Sam had by now discreetly coughed up his latest piece of cake in anticipation of its getting stuck in his throat, and despite the ravages of his hangover, was starting to have a bit of fun as he watched the detective try to get out of the old lady what the purpose of her telephone call was. Bradley, for his part, asked with more than a touch of misgiving.

Emily showed no stress or anxiety at the depredations of the filth spread over her front yard. She did have, after all, as Sam saw through a window on the other side of the room, a back garden of about twenty acres. But there was something in Emily's eyes as she stared dreamily out over the rooftops that made him think she had either just ingested a mood-controlling drug, or, more surprisingly, that she was capable of focusing on an object in the middle distance. Sam became sensible of a strange thudding noise just as her phone rang. Without moving her eyes from the heavens, she answered it.

'That's it, Terence, my lad. You've got it. You *are* a good boy! Yes, that's the one. Try not to hit the next-door house – the one with the garden covered in sewage – that's my place and I'd hate to miss the show by being collateral damage.'

'My godson,' she said, ringing off, and looking blithely at the men. 'He's stationed at the military airbase a few miles south of the town. He assured me that if it was needed, he could loose off a few rounds and blame it on a malfunction.'

Emily's face had taken on an almost beatific aspect by this point, staring out of the window as the thudding noise grew to a pitch that defied speech and a gigantic helicopter lowered into view through the window, its wings under-clustered with tree-trunk missiles and fridge-wide rocket launchers.

'I think we should leave,' said Sam, much too late, as bright shimmering blasts were followed by clods of earth being flung up in the air, accompanied by the noise of the garden next door having a sequence of three-feet-deep holes plunged into it and its vegetable contents distributed all over the surrounding streets in fine ash.

Sam, witnessing these events and unsure for a moment which of his many reactions he should act upon, at last rugby-tackled Emily to the ground, and in one diving movement first swallowed, then choked on, and at last ejected a final chunk of cake.

Emily responded gratefully, by kneeing him at once hard in the bollocks and jumping back up to watch the carnage, shouting encouragements at the window, and shielding her face from the shattering glass with the lace curtain.

Looking around, Sam saw that the detective was well ahead of him in escaping this mad scenario – he had crawled to the back door, and was gesturing for him to follow.

Chapter Six

'So,' BRADLEY SAID once they had crawled to safety, waited for the gun smoke to lift and at last regained their car. 'Village life is boring, is it?'

'Yes,' said Sam, whose adrenalin, now he was comfortably sitting down, had most definitely ebbed, to be replaced by his hangover. And a good deal of irritation. 'Yes, it *is* boring. With the occasional exception of sudden episodes of psychopathic lunacy. Don't try and teach me a lesson – I feel like shit. Give me that bottle . . .' He swigged three painkillers with some water and then stared out of the window, putting on a more than slightly childish expression.

Bradley was in contrast temporarily bucked-up by his near-death experience, and his realization that there were plenty of motives in the town that might have contributed to Mr Fairbreath's disappearance, from the Quimples' insane drop-of-a-hat murderousness, to the potentially life-changing issues at stake in the Parish Council vote, in which he was the lynchpin. He was starting to feel as though he could be on the scent.

'There's an emergency council meeting at three p.m. today,' he said. 'They're going to discuss Terry's replacement. It might give us an insight into other people's feelings about him.'

'Right,' said Sam grumpily. 'Why do they have to act so fast?'

'There was a big meeting that came up the week he went missing – they were to vote on a series of very important issues. Apparently Terry had the "swing" vote, so to speak. The future of the town may be at stake.' Bradley consulted his watch. 'But we've got lots of time before then. We should speak to a few more of the council members.'

'So who next, then? The butcher, the baker, the candlestick maker?'

'Apparently the candlestick maker is in the South of France at this time of year, so he's out. Lord Selvington mentioned we should visit Major Eldred,' said Bradley, suddenly becoming much quieter. 'He's a bit potty, but I suppose we should strike him off the list. And you never know what mad people are ready to tell you, that ordinary people wouldn't.'

'Yes, good point,' said Sam, at first not listening, but then realizing the detective's voice had fallen to a whisper.

'I don't remember feeling this vile since my wedding

day,' said Bradley, holding his leather-gloved hands up so they shook violently.

'Your mates gave you a pretty heavy stag do, did they?' asked Sam, smiling.

'Stag *what*? No, certainly not,' said Bradley, irritated, and gunning the engine, he took them in a sickeningly swerving route to the major's house.

Even if the two men weren't already feeling somewhat weary from last night's consumption of alcohol, after the major's performance at the council meeting the previous day they would still have had heavy hearts when they found themselves pulling the bell of his diminutive cottage. This sensation grew even worse when the sound greeting them was the blast of a foghorn that scattered all the birds from the copse of ash trees at the summit of the hill half a mile away.

'*What?*' said the major, leaning out of an upper window.

'We've come to see you,' said Bradley.

'Oh,' said the major. 'Right.' He looked out over the countryside from his vantage point and squinted. 'Nice day, isn't it?'

'Not really,' said Sam.

'Hmm, hmm. The cricket's on later, you know?'

'Is it really?' said Bradley, clearly at a loss for anything else to say.

'Can we come in, please?' said Sam.

'Oh!' said the major, the idea clearly striking him as rather novel. 'Er . . . yes.' And he disappeared from the window, only to appear again a moment later, shouting, 'LOOK OUT!' as a bowlful of brown lumpy liquid fell directly at them.

They jumped apart and examined their trousers (although Bradley's were already so daubed with brown slop, it would have been hard to tell if anything had been added to the overall design). Then they looked up, in disbelief, to find the major's face staring out at them.

'Goulash,' he pronounced shortly, before he disappeared again and descended the stairs, coughing violently. Then the door popped open and he said, 'Come in, come in!' ushering them cheerfully through the living room, which was full of dust, furniture piled up with old boxes, huge nineteenth-century firearms propped against the wall and (as far as Sam could make out) a painting of a bison's arse above the fireplace.

The kitchen offered few surprises – which is to say, it would have been a surprise had it been a clean, orderly and well-appointed place whose fittings dated from more recently than the Falklands War. All around there were rusty pans hanging from nails – evidently unused, since there was a bird's nest in one of them – and on the hob was a gargantuan stock pot filled with a very large sheep's head, marinating in what smelled like cider.

Sam sat at a solid old-fashioned cook's table, whose top was marked with wild scratches and carvings, some of which included unpleasant words and simplistic imagery.

'I'll get you some refreshment,' the major said, disappearing into his pantry for ten minutes, from whence emerged strange noises which they felt they couldn't investigate. At last the madman reappeared and plonked three bowls of custard on the table.

'For my guests,' said the major, and before they could respond he poured a bottle of crème de menthe into three pint-pots and handed them out.

'We're here—' began Bradley, but not quick enough, for the major now stood, raised a bugle to his lips and played a shrieking rendition of the last post. Finally he sat down again, wiping a sad tear from his one good eye.

'Come on, sunshine,' said Sam. 'You can give it a rest with us.'

'Eh?' asked the major, twisting his face somewhere between a scowl and a look of utter incomprehension.

'You're not actually mad. Anyone can see.'

The major seemed determined to be affronted for a second, but then relented and relaxed, and said in a quite ordinary voice, 'Oh, all right. But so long as you don't tell anyone. What gave me away?'

'Well, you're wearing your eyepatch on the other eye today, for starters.'

'Hah! I knew I'd got something wrong. That's the trouble with being startled by the doorbell – which is why I give it such a repugnant noise.'

'And you're three quarters of the way through this *Guardian* cryptic crossword here.'

'I'm impressed. You've looked closely enough to see that the answers are correct?'

'Well, no . . .' admitted Sam, looking down.

'Hah – now you're wondering if the answer to sixteen across really could be "pissbucket". But then, it is the *Guardian*. They'd probably run that as a title to a children's cartoon, just to confront old-fashioned attitudes to swearing.'

'But I guessed that if you were going to fill the crossword with nonsense, why stop halfway through? And also, what self-respecting, warmongering retired major would be reading the *Guardian* in the first place . . .'

'Fair enough,' said the major.

'And what about the sheep's head?' asked Sam.

'It's plastic.'

Sam started to look closer, but it was so convincing that in his hungover state he couldn't bear to do so. 'And the painting of the buffalo's arse?' he asked.

'The *what*? You terrible bastard, that's my *wife*!'

Sam didn't have any idea what to say back and instead

looked around the room, avoiding the major's goggle-eyed stare.

'So why the act?' asked Bradley, intervening.

'Oh well, you know. People around here are so *boring*. You were at the meeting. What did you see?'

The guests were unsure if they were really being asked to reply.

Instead the major quickly answered for himself: 'Prudes, freaks, prats, bores, virgins, thickos, creeps and fucking *Tories*! No wonder I pretend to be mad. Last thing I want is them charging in here and disturbing my peace. Talking of which, let's not stay in this freak show of a room – this is just to put off someone who gets as far as the kitchen. Come on, let's go through here.'

He reached forward to a bookshelf at the far end of the room and pressed on the spine of *The Essays of Montaigne*, releasing a secret door. Within was a library-cum-sitting room, sparsely furnished with a Mac on a table, an architect's desk, a low sofa with a few chairs and several thousand books on dark-wood shelves.

'You're an architect?' asked Sam.

'It's a hobby. Mostly small buildings for exclusive clients. I also write a blog about riverside wildlife and I'm a main player in the longest-running online game of *Dungeons and Dragons* in the world. Life's pretty sweet sometimes, you know, when you're retired . . .'

'So why be on the Parish Council?' asked Bradley, sitting down. 'Surely that's putting yourself into the lion's den, so to speak? Or the lion's mouth, do I mean?'

'Neither. The last thing I want is to hand the management of the community entirely over to these cretins. Well, you saw for yourself yesterday the kind of crap that they come out with. I wanted to make sure I always vote for the most sensible course, and goad others into following me.'

'Even if your reasoning seems insane?'

'Yes, exactly.'

'So you must be worried about Terry Fairbreath going missing. If you're a Tory-hater he must have been an ally.'

'Certainly he was. A nice normal fellow, always around except when he went to visit his mother once a month. He was an excellent chess partner too. And with this vote coming up . . .'

'So tell us what the vote's about.'

'They want to build a wind farm near here.'

'And no doubt Lord Selvington's saying, "Not in my back yard"?'

'Yes, but literally, because it *is* in his back yard. They would look directly down onto his property and apparently take about three million pounds off its worth. Which, when all's said and done, is quite a lot. Don't let the mannered pleasantness of the meetings fool you, there are matters of life and death at stake. Then there are the Miss Quimples . . .'

'Ah yes, we just visited them. They keep accidentally causing violence on each other's gardens.'

'That's them. They're opposed to anything new.'

'What exactly do they class as new?' asked Bradley. 'Video games? Colour television?'

'Bumming?' put in Sam.

'Bumming's definitely out. But the Internet, *especially* the Internet.'

'Ha!' Bradley laughed. 'Well, I don't suppose they've had much luck in banning *that*.'

'Don't you believe it. China could learn a thing or two. There's still no WiFi in the village.'

Sam toggled with his phone and realized it was true; he barely had any reception.

'I don't suppose that's a problem for you . . .'

'Are you kidding?' the major frothed. 'It completely fucks with livestreaming the fucking podcast. And with my online fucking poker. (It doesn't exactly help my online fucking, either).'

Sam blinked and pretended he hadn't heard the last remark. 'You, uh, you play online poker?'

''Course I do, how else is a pensioner supposed to make up his winter fuel allowance in Blair's Britain?'

'It's not actually Blair's Britain any more.'

'Isn't it? Oh well, whomever. Obviously things were better under Major. Just 'cause of the name, you know?' He winked at Sam, whom he clearly took to be a kindred spirit, perhaps on account of the fact that he had brought both the crème de menthe and the bowl of custard with him, and was cradling the latter in his lap.

'What's their problem with WiFi?' Sam asked, now taking a taste from the tip of a spoon of custard.

'They said they thought it caused tumours.'

'Who would know what causes tumours in these folks? They're all a hundred and three anyway . . .' said Sam.

'We're getting off the point,' said Bradley, looking at his watch. 'We've got other council members to get to. I just wanted to ask, Major—'

'I'm not a major, actually.'

'*Mister* Eldred, then . . .'

'As a matter of fact, I'm a Doctor of Oriental Languages.'

'Doctor, then. Do you know of any reason why anyone would want Terry Fairbreath to disappear?'

'Six of them,' he said cheerfully.

'Would you please elucidate?'

'One: there was a rumour he had an affair with – what's his name? The artist. I can never remember it. Aloysius something.'

'Walerian Exosius. He shagged that guy?'

'No – his sister, so the rumour went. When she came to stay last spring.'

'Is it true?'

'No, no, no! Terry's camper than the Brighton male all-nude self-raising tent Olympics. Unless it's all just an act, of course, and he's shagging prostitutes behind our backs. Hah! But the artist doesn't realize that he's gay, so he swore revenge on Terry, based on rumour alone. Second reason . . .' he counted them off on his fingers, 'he unknowingly picked Miss Quimple's aubergines over those of her sister when he was a judge at last year's flower show. He said they were remarkable – plump and firm and sensual, and he wanted to put his hands all over them. But he said it to the wrong sister, you see. She nearly fainted. It was the highlight of my summer. Then he picked *that* sister's melons over the other and made the same mistake all over again. So they both hate him.'

'As well as having access to explosives and firearms,' pointed out Bradley. 'What did he say about the melons?'

'Oh, let me see, I did write it down . . .' Both men smiled at his presumed joke, but then he produced a small black notebook and, flicking the pages back, said, 'Ah yes, here we are: "Squeezy, sumptuous – I want to have their juices running down my chin." Yuck! He really was an unassuageable pervert. But then, who isn't in this day and age? How's the custard?'

Sam nodded happily, a spoonful still to his lips.

'Fourth on the list: the mayor. Another pervert. A man

who is a pathetic, short-statured, poorly organized, self-aggrandizing, bad excuse for a public official, but who is really just a twat . . .'

'What do you mean by that, exactly?' asked Bradley, paused with his pen over his notebook.

'Sorry if I wasn't being clear,' said the major, clearing his throat, and flicking up his eyepatch. 'What I meant was that he is . . . a *twat*.'

'In this usage,' said Sam from his seat behind the detective, 'I think the word means a useless or risibly pointless person.'

'I see,' said Bradley. 'What are the final two reasons?'

'Reason five: he was in charge of the local movement to oppose military installations nearby.'

'What military installations?'

'They had a couple of thousand intercontinental ballistic missiles stationed about ten miles away until a few years ago and the locals revolted, got them out. The idea was to stockpile about a thousand weapons beneath the great Hill at the top of town. Along with Saracene Galaxista, Terry opposed this and got backing from lots of people.'

Sam was halfway through sipping his bowl of crème de menthe-flavoured custard, which was filling his stomach with warmish velvety goodness ('Like a crap hot version of Baileys,' he thought to himself), but he still made a mental note that he must try and persuade Bradley that their next interview should take place in the pub. For entertainment value, at the very least. It then occurred to him that he was taking the matter of a man who was missing and possibly murdered very lightly. *Then* it occurred to him that he was drinking alcoholic mint-flavoured custard from a bowl, and spilling some of it down his top, and he should try to deal with one thing at a time.

'Final reason: he was sniffing around. He had been quite excited these last few weeks and months. He was the sort of chap who'd love to expose a miscarriage of justice, or a cover up of some kind and he kept hinting at it. Not heavy-handed hints, you understand, but accidentally. He was foraging around in the library recently, and seemed to have a bee in his bonnet. This vote, for instance – it was supposed to be passed six weeks ago but he kept having it delayed while he asked for extra time to look into some-thing. People were wary enough of him already, but that might have been what tipped someone over the edge.'

The two men were intrigued and excited by this last possibility.

'What do you think he was looking for?' asked Bradley.

'I couldn't possibly tell you,' said their host. 'Remember, I've only been here a few years – less time than him.'

'We've got lots of motives to investigate, then,' said Bradley. 'I suppose we ought to speak to some of these folks as soon as we can. Thank you, Major – I mean, Doctor.'

'That's okay,' he said, getting up. 'Good luck. I hope you liked the custard.'

'It was pretty good,' said Sam, wiping the last from his mouth with his sleeve. 'Thanks very much.'

'Pleasure. Never met someone else who likes custard made from tortoise milk before. I'll cook some more for you next time.'

The major (or doctor) saw them to the door, closed it and then watched with amusement through the spyhole as Sam ran to one side to avoid being ungrateful to his host and vomited a violent gutful of grey custard onto next door's lawn.

'It's not yet twelve, so we've still got a good while to go before the emergency Parish Council meeting this afternoon,' said Bradley. 'How's the hangover?'

'Pretty awful,' said Sam, then gargled with water from a bottle. 'Surely we've done enough of these old duffers for a morning? Can't we go out into the country?'

Bradley looked at his watch. 'Yes, I suppose so,' he said. 'Who do you think we should speak to, then?'

'The druid. They say she lives up here on the Hill.'

'Okay, then,' said Bradley, nodding, and just at the same moment he spotted his police car up the road where he'd left it the night before, clicked the button to turn off the alarm with a triumphant gesture, danced a little jig and trotted up to it.

'You shouldn't do that,' said Sam, following twenty yards behind.

'What?'

'You shouldn't ask me where we should go next, for starters. But you certainly shouldn't do a little dance when the car alarm release goes off, like you're on a game show.'

'Oh what*ever*,' said Bradley, unlocking the door.

There was a sudden loud boom from nearby that made them both stop speaking, and look to where a plume of smoke was rising from the grounds of the school. No ordinary smoke, however, because this was green and giving off showers of blue sparks.

'My God,' said Bradley. 'Some sort of terrible explosion at the school!'

'Don't worry,' said a voice, and they spotted a schoolmaster further down the lane. He was looking particularly bedraggled, his trousers hanging in shreds and his face covered in soot. 'Just a, uh, just a science experiment!' he called out, sounding rather nervous. 'No need to come and investigate – none at all! Good day! Oh dear . . .'

And with that the strange man (who bore a remarkable resemblance to the actor Jim Broadbent) tottered out of view, back into the school grounds.

'Is there *anything* that doesn't explode around here?' asked Sam, and both men walked slowly off towards the car, casting suspicious glances over their shoulders as they went.

Chapter Seven

SAM WAITED UNTIL they had been driving for a few minutes before he raised the topic again.

'I really think you need to be a bit more . . . you know,' he said.

'I feel I know what you're getting at,' said Bradley. 'I should be more of a, er, a sort of . . . rough type.' The detective had been leaning forward and clutching the steering wheel nervously but now he forced himself to lean back into his seat and put his foot down, making the speed surge. 'You were going to say I wasn't enough of a man; that I should be more aggressive.'

'Hey, listen! When we're alone in the car there's nothing to gain by you being a macho cop – God damn it, slow down! I'm feeling G-force here. Mind that— My God, did we hit it? Okay, that's it, slower, *slower*. Okay, so the one thing I was going to say was, be more hardball in all your dealings with humans – apart from me.'

'Define hardball,' said Bradley, taking his eyes off the road and gunning the acceleration once more.

Sam was happy to give out advice, but in his current state (and in fact, in *any* state whatsoever) he was not content to have his life put at risk simply for the purposes of making a drive in the country slightly more brisk. He made his feelings on this subject clear in words of one syllable.

'Don't take me as an example,' he said. 'But here's my advice. Take no shit from no one, and refuse to believe what anyone says unless they've got cast-iron proof to back it up. Beat the crap out of the strong and threaten the weak mercilessly, then toss them a few crumbs of relief afterwards for the illusion that you wouldn't fuck them over next time. Don't trust your boss. Screw the system, and fuck being trustworthy except by your own twisted code – will you *stop?*'

Bradley braked sharply then came to a slewing halt in the middle of a car-park clearing in the centre of the woods.

'That's good,' said Sam, puking out of the window. 'You're doing well. I've never . . . I've never praised someone while puking before,' he added. 'And I guess I'm all the more impressed for that fact.'

As Bradley went up ahead to the encampment on the top of the hill, Sam decided to remain seated on a tree stump in the woods, claiming he wanted to check for emails on his phone while still in signal, but in fact (as would have been clear to anyone more experienced in life than Bradley), he had been badly caught short and was nervously watching passing traffic for an opportunity to take an unde-tected toilet break in the woods.

As Bradley neared the crest of the hill, he was braced by a quickening breeze, and coming closer to the top he found that the grasses swept in the high wind like gentle waves. The treeline parted, the bright sky broadened massively about him, and here, far away from the duties to which he was accustomed, and the life he knew, he suddenly and unexpectedly saw the beauty of the landscape as if for the first time, which quite took his breath away.

'Oh, it's you, you twat!' said a voice.

He turned and saw a middle-aged hag in thick boots trudging up the hill towards him.

'Saracene Galaxista,' he said. She stopped and he saw the reason for her bad temper and stooping gait. 'Let me help you with that,' he offered.

'Oh, go on, then,' she muttered, and handed over the twin pails of milk she was carrying. 'Maybe you're not that bad, despite being a pig. I'm only one of the order of Sisters of Galaxista. We're just over here.'

Bradley soon had cause to regret his largesse. For some reason when he made the remark it felt like holding open a door for a lady, a marginally meaningful gesture. Where had he assumed her to be taking the milk to – a meeting with him upon this random tussock? In fact, it turned out to be the camp a quarter of a mile away over some decidedly squelchy uplands about which Mrs Detective would certainly have something to say when it came to the effects on his Marks & Spencer brogues.

That is little, however, compared to the effect that it had on his state of mind. A hangover which had been largely in retreat now made huge gains in important areas of head pain, nervousness, weariness, self-hatred and weakness to suggestion, and after Bradley had planted the milk down he passed out for a couple of minutes leaning against a goat, only waking to discover that Sam had caught up with him.

'You were crying in your sleep,' said Sam. 'That *is* a bad hangover.'

'Where's she gone?' said Bradley. 'Why is it wherever I go, I only get to talk to you?'

'That's the spirit.' Sam punched him in the leg. 'I was thinking,' he said, 'that if I'm going to be stuck in this village or town, or what have you for the next few days, I'm probably going to need whatever sustenance I can get to keep me going. I'm assuming you've never smoked weed?'

Bradley smiled as though this were a trick question, because to him the idea of a policeman taking drugs of any kind was a genuinely amusing idea – like a nun going to the toilet. It simply didn't happen. Meanwhile the woman they were there to interview came back from a nearby tent, smiled briefly at Bradley, turned her back on him and started a mumbling conversation with Sam.

'I'm not *made* of money . . .' said Sam, followed by, '. . . Yes, that's good. Okay, nice . . . No, come on, I've got to draw the line *somewhere* and horse tranquilizers is it . . .'

Some money changed hands and then they separated, both looking very pleased and placing things deep into their pockets, before they realized that the detective was watching them intently.

'Thank God I found you,' said Sam too loudly to the druid. 'I don't know what I would be able to do without my herbal tea remedies.'

Bradley looked the other two up and down.

'How can I help you?' asked Saracene Galaxista.

'I want to know who would have wanted Terry Fairbreath out of the way,' he said, bad temperedly.

'That fucker? Everyone,' she replied. 'Come into my tent.'

SHE SERVED them both with a cup of tea in a tent that was, much to their surprise, far more like a tasteful ordinary British drawing room than Major Eldred's had been. Galaxista was hard to make out – she seemed half stupid, half bored and half stoned. And half *intelligent*, Bradley kept thinking to himself, but then he knew that was possibly a stupid remark to make, even inside your own head, so he abandoned it.

'They all hated him, as you say. The little old sisters, the stupid fat Mayor, the Reverend, Lord Selvington, even the librarian.'

'The *librarian*?'

'Yes. Miss Elvesdon, that decided weirdo. They became friends – study pals, bosom buddies – over something. I think they were digging up something from the past. Then when he called it to a halt she was very hurt. You know, you should probably seek out the only heterosexual single male in the village, they would probably have a grudge against dear Terry. He was gay as a cock-shaped kite on the Queen's Jubilee, but women swarmed to him.'

Bradley nodded and took this in, but was not ignorant of the extended roll-up that was being passed around. He didn't know enough about that sort of thing to make trouble, and he was still reliant on Sam to tell him how to develop his act. And Sam was having most of the roll-up, as far as he could tell.

'So, who wanted Terry killed, Sister Galaxista?' he asked.

'Sorry, love,' said the sister, sitting back on a cushion

next to him. 'It's more a case of who *didn't* want him killed. By which I mean me, *I* didn't. He was a sweetheart for us and our cause.'

'And what *is* your cause?'

'We started off objecting to the nuclear waste dumps they were planning here thirty-five years ago,' she explained. 'Then there was going to be a massive bypass right across the hill, near the henge, and we said, like, *no*. No way! We got enough people and we rejected it.'

'So you succeeded?' Bradley asked.

'Yes, but they keep on trying,' said Saracene. 'Their latest plan is to dump thousands of unused books here. A bunch of publishers had tens of thousands of those crappy parodies – you know, when talentless half-brained hacks try to make a quick buck off the back of genuinely successful authors by writing things with similar titles and book covers?' she spat on the floor. 'It makes me sick. Anyway, they have hundreds of tonnes of these knock-off books they want to get rid of, and they want to dig a hole in the hill here and bury them. But we said no. We cannot let it happen. You understand?'

'Yes, we understand,' said Sam. 'You really don't want it to happen.'

'No. It *can't* happen. This is a place of outstanding natural beauty, of ancient wonderment. We will call all the land's children here to procreate and worship beneath the henge!'

'Procreate?' said Sam, starting to find his proximity to Galaxista uncomfortable. He sniffed suspiciously at his tea. 'What's in this exactly?' he asked.

'Just tea,' she smiled.

'And milk?'

'Tortoise milk, of course,' she said. 'It's full of complex proteins.' He threw it on the floor with a shout.

'Henge?' Bradley was saying. 'Oh, I see. It really is a place of crucial heritage.'

'Stones came here from hundreds of miles away. This isn't just a gathering of people who happen to be here and who reject modern technology. This is an ancient place of worship where ancient rituals are enacted by present-day people. Big, important rituals!'

'Right,' said Bradley. 'Sam, let go of my arm. Sorry, go on. So what do you guys do up here, is there some kind of ritual?'

'Oh, yes. And look here,' she pointed out of a gap in the side of the tent. 'We have forty men, women and children working with wicker all day long. They are helping to make our main piece for the great sacrifice.'

'How remarkable. And it's shaped like an enormous pole, almost like a man's p— Sam! Stop tugging my arm like that!'

'And here we have sixty others, digging the ceremonial trench . . .'

'I see, I see. Almost like a woman's . . . Yes, Sam. don't worry, I'm coming with you. Let's hurry along now. So long, sister! Put that cigarette down, now, Sam. Run!'

Chapter Eight

SAM SNOOZED OFF the effects of his large cigarette on the way back to the town, and when woken up on arriving there, he insisted on getting some lunch.

'Not just *any* lunch,' he said. 'Let's get some proper lunch.'

Detective Inspector Bradley soon gave up trying to suggest what a proper lunch might be, allowing Sam's nose to follow itself until they stumbled across the Legume & Gastropod pub, tucked away in a winding side alley.

'Garlic mushrooms,' said Sam, before his backside had even touched the bench. 'Onion rings, deep-fried whitebait and a bacon-triple-cheeseburger. With onions, relish and anything else that comes with it. And a Coke? I would come in and order with you but I've got a bad leg.' He handed the menu back to Bradley with a twenty-pound note, fell back in a swoon against the leather chair, turned his face to the window and relaxed in the hot sunshine.

'Ordered,' said Bradley, appearing sooner than expected.

'Okay, man,' said the writer, who, with the promise of

large amounts of juicy fried food coming his way, surprised himself by snapping out of his reverie. 'How do you think this is going? I'm getting a big kick out of this, baby.'

'I . . . I'm not sure,' said Bradley, picking over his words carefully. 'I'm concerned that you were dealing drugs with those crusties up there . . .' he began.

'Good,' encouraged Sam.

'But then, I'm also slightly terrified that if we'd stayed up there long enough they would have sacrificed us to the sun god.'

'It must be quite close to some solstice or other,' said Sam. 'And notice how I gave you a helpful wrist-tugging hint . . .'

'Gold star to you there, young man,' said Bradley, who was pleased to see that his approbation gave Sam pleasure. 'Well done for saving our lives,' he reiterated. 'But still it leaves a lot unexplained. And still more motives!'

'Hmm,' said Sam, sipping his Coke. 'We've still got to talk to the mayor, and many others, but I think we should get hold of the man with the Ye Olde Shoppe.'

'Yes, he certainly sounds like he has a grudge against the council, that could be a motive.'

'Right,' said Sam, caught off-guard. 'He has a motive, all right. But he's also missing out on some *major* other Dickens puns for his shop.'

'Right, I see—'

'Nicholas Nippleby, A Tale of Two Titties, David Cop-a-feel. That's off the top of my head, if he wants to have a porn shop. If he wants to get into any other linem of business (except being an actual Old Curiosity Shop), I could come up with a dozen puns on the spot.'

As Bradley was in the course of nodding and smiling, and agreeing in order to stop Sam speaking, their food arrived and they quickly settled into companionable silence. Sam's wordplay was happily confined to the *Guardian* easy crossword, while Bradley was rereading the *Daily Mail* that he had got all the way through at breakfast. By the time their food had been taken away and they were finishing their drinks, DI Bradley was looking at his watch.

'It's nearly time for the Parish Council meeting,' he said sadly.

'Right,' said Sam, leaping to his feet. 'I'm just going to very quickly nip to the bar. . .'

BRADLEY AND SAM were admitted early to the meeting this time, although admittedly both were slightly nodding their heads owing to the 'restorative' double shots of whisky Sam had bought them both. However, it took the other members so long to assemble, and the room was so cool and shady and (with its many tall windows covered in dusty drapes) so deadening to sound, that the two men had the helpful best part of a half-hour's rest at the back of the room before the meeting commenced.

'We're here today to discuss another member joining us,' said Lord Selvington, snapping the room to attention. The detective and his companion instinctively looked at Major Eldred, who eyed them both meaningfully in turn before switching his gaze to the chairman. 'And this is a very important decision. I suppose, beforehand – Miss Stissinghurst, is there anything we really need to get off the minutes from yesterday?'

'I'm afraid,' came a rather prim and schoolmarmish voice, 'that we still have the issue of Cedric's shop.'

'Oh, bugger it,' whispered Lord Selvington audibly, and a big grin spread over Major Eldred's face.

'This is the issue that we have tried to prevent Cedric Gray . . .' said Selvington.

'. . . Cedric the Bastard,' said Saracene Galaxista.

'I'm *aware* what he changed his name to,' said Selvington in a warning tone.

'It's deed poll, you can't not call him it.'

'Fine,' said Selvington, running a hand over his forehead. 'The man who used to be called Cedric Gray, and who—'

'And who is now called Cedric the Bastard . . .' said Major Eldred.

'Fine,' said Selvington. 'Fine! Call him what you want.

Does someone else want to take over the relentless brain-fuck of handling this meeting?'

Major Eldred and Saracene Galaxista were enjoying themselves hugely but not enough to want to actually take over, so they lowered their eyes.

'Oh! No? No one else? Listen, Cedric can change his name on deed poll to "Fuck the Parish Council Meeting in the Quivering Arsehole" if he likes, I still have to get through the agenda. So, item one, here's a huge bloody surprise, Cedric the Tedious Flippin' Bastard's shop has changed its name. Yes?'

'Yes,' said the quiet voice of the Parish secretary from the corner.

'I know we in this meeting, and in this village, have long had a problem with Cedric's shop being called Ye The Olde Curiositye Shoppe. We've had a vote on every one of those extra letters. Except perhaps for that extra "p", which we didn't object to after allowing the "e" that went with it.'

There was a brief pause while everyone took this in, not just the two visitors to the chamber.

'Please tell me,' said Lord Selvington, 'that he has decided, as we have long demanded of him, to remove either the "Ye" or the "The".'

'No, he wants to change the "Ye" into a "Yeay" – Y, E, A, Y. To make it more phonetic.'

'It doesn't have to be more *phonetic*, it's a fucking sign!'

'But for Americans. That's what he's saying.'

'It's even worse than before,' chipped in one of the Quimples. 'That's like text speak.'

'Exactly,' said the major, his one visible eye goggling. 'Why are we troubled by this runt, week after week? Is he English at all?'

'He *is* called Cedric.'

'Are Cedrics really English? Sounds a bit Danish. I mean, is it illegal to kill the bleeders?'

There was a considerable amount of gasping at this, which only encouraged the major to rise to his theme. 'I mean to say, and I have been hoping to get the phrase "I mean to say" in for quite a while, so God damn it, I mean to say it!' he said. 'We have to talk about this crapulous little buffoon's signposting habits for almost half the meeting every week and I Mean To Say I resent that it delays me getting my cup of bloody tea and Rich Tea (or WHATEVER) biscuit. So there.' And so saying he stood back down from the table and removed the scimitar he had thrust passionately through the ornaments in the top of Miss E. Quimple's hat, which might once have resembled fruit or birds, but were now snowflakes of paper.

'Thank you, Major,' said Lord Selvington quietly, 'for moving the conversation on so far as to discuss Cedric's name.'

'May I for my part say,' said the mayor, already looking

quite pleased with himself, 'if he wants it to be in text speak, why doesn't he go the whole hog and call it Yeay, The Olde Curiosity Shoppe Lol!'

'Well, exactly,' said Emily Quimple.

'No, that was a joke,' said the mayor, with a falling face.

'OMG ROFLMAO!' said Sam suddenly from the corner, at the top of his voice, smiling.

They all turned slowly to look at him in confusion, including the mayor (looking more scornful than the others, clearly grateful to have the attention distracted from himself) and once again he found how unexpectedly out of place he was among these rich old folks. He was surprised at how abashed he felt.

'WTF,' Sam muttered to himself, leaning back into the shadows.

'Well, apparently it's "Yeay" or "Thee" with two "e"s, and that's that.'

'For crap's sake, it doesn't make any sense,' said Lord Selvington. 'What is he, on commission from the Unconvincing Old-Fashioned Font Association? No. Our answer is no. What's next on the agenda?'

'It's the least curious shop I've ever seen, anyway,' said the Reverend Smallcreak. 'It's just full of *tat*.'

'Point two, a question from two meetings ago, when I wasn't taking the minutes,' came the voice of Lord Selvington's secretary. 'Re: the opening of the £7 million abbey renovation. Are we *really* to invite Abi Titmuss to cut the cord?'

Selvington gave the mayor a suspicious glance.

'I don't *think* so,' protested that dignitary, evidently very excited and shifting in his seat. 'Did we *really* say that?'

'Apparently she came top of the list,' said the one-eyed major sadly, reading from his minutes. 'I suppose it's because she's called Abi,' he said, looking up. 'And has huge knockers.'

'Well, I must say Abi Titmuss is a charming name,' said one of the Quimples. 'Sounds like a type of bird.'

'She certainly *is* a type of bird, but not one of which you would approve, possibly,' said the major, leaning back in his chair, looking pleased with himself.

'Oh dear,' said the other Miss Quimple, looking distressed. 'Not a *chaffinch*?'

'I fear we're straying from the point somewhat,' said Lord Selvington slightly huffily. 'Let us return to this next time, Miss Stissinghurst. Now, ladies and gentlemen, of course we all hope Terry is going to turn up alive and well as soon as possible but he is not here, and as we all know, with our vote coming up at the end of this week, and the votes standing the way they are, we need to fill up this vacancy (which is, in the circumstances, not so much of a "casual vacancy" as we would hope it might be). So it is now time for us to meet our candidates . . .'

'Time for refreshments, then,' said the major, in such an excitement that he switched his eyepatch from one socket to the other without anyone but Sam noticing. Tea was indeed brought, poured and handed round, with Custard Cream biscuits on each saucer.

'Please bring the first one in, Mrs Trench,' said the mayor, and the frightening and apparently female creature who had welcomed Sam and Bradley in the previous day limped theatrically to the door, pulled it open and then nodded to whoever was outside.

Sam found this woman chillingly fascinating, in just the same way that he would sometimes catch a glimpse of a particularly unwell and miserable-looking homeless person, or someone in the furthest stages of a degenerative disease, and be suddenly convinced that by some cruel and relatively sudden twist of fate he might find himself in their shoes. These occasional shocks were one of the relatively few things that genuinely gave his existence zest and meaning. She seemed to have not much more mental faculty than the average home computer, and accomplished her simple tasks with a great deal of visible effort. She presently subsided onto a chair at the back of the room and instantly fell asleep, farting loudly as she did so.

This was quite possibly a common enough occurrence not to warrant any notice or comment from anyone else in the council, but either way their attention was now firmly fixed on their first interviewee. He was a tall man, fat and completely bald, perhaps fifty years old, and wearing blue jeans and a white T-shirt with a picture of the Union Jack on it.

'Now,' said Lord Selvington, clearing his throat and looking at the papers in front of him, 'I understand that you were until recently Professor of Middle Eastern Politics at Trinity College Dublin, is that right?'

'Nah, nah,' said the man, waving his hand. 'I run a burger van.'

'Oh, I'm so sorry,' said Selvington, putting the paper down. 'I was getting you mixed up with Angharad Trefusis.'

'Who, in turn, must be a woman,' said the mayor quietly.

'Er, indeed. Please do go on,' said Selvington.

'Well, I run my burger van just up on the A-road over the hill, and what I'm saying is . . .'

'I'm sorry,' said Selvington. 'You actually *live* here in Mumford?'

'That's right,'

He nodded three times.

'*Really?*'

The man nodded again.

'Good *Lord*,' said Selvington.

'I'm not a racist . . .' began their guest.

'Now, wait a minute. Call me old mister psychologypants,' said the mayor, 'but that probably means that you *are*, doesn't it? Just a bit.'

'No! No, what I'm saying is – and hear me out – is that I think we should keep this town the way it is, and – excuse my French – but not let in any bloody foreigners.'

'There we go,' muttered the mayor. 'I owe myself a fiver. Clever old psychologypants.'

'But my dear man, there *aren't* any foreigners,' said Selvington. 'That's why the property prices are so high, and we're one of the country's most famous and desirable towns.'

'I'm not a racist,' insisted the man again. 'I like Bolognese, and curry and that.'

'Yes, yes, that's fine. Thank you – we've got lots more people to see today, so would you mind making way for our next candidate . . .'

The man lumbered disappointedly out of the room and the mayor and Selvington both shouted together to wake Mrs Trench to invite the next guest in.

The next man strode in confidently, a wide fellow with an enormous bushy beard, bright eyes and the ruddy complexion of someone who shouted a great deal.

'Looks like Brian Blessed,' muttered Sam to himself.

'I am indeed the famous actor Brian Blessed!' yelled the man. 'I would like to join your Parish Council.'

'Brian, we've had this discussion a dozen times. You're not getting in.'

'Why not?' bellowed the enormous actor.

'Because you're a lovely fellow, but the one time we had you in here, we got nothing done.'

'Remind me?' enquired Blessed at the top of his voice, suspiciously.

'You mutter under your breath and it's very off-putting.'

'Plain nonsense!' foghorned Blessed. The actor looked round at Sam and Bradley, raising his eyebrows and then jerked his thumb at Selvington as if to say, 'Look at this fellow!'

'*What* do I mutter?' he demanded.

Selvington took off his glasses and rubbed the top of his nose. 'Must we do this? We all know where it's going.'

'I will not be oppressed, you vermin! Tell me! What is the phrase?' And he cocked a hand against his ear and turned the ear towards the chairman, with an expression of majestic fascination, like a king listening for the trumpet-call of victory from a far beacon-post.

'It's extraordinary,' whispered Bradley. 'He really does shout *all the time!*'

'"Gordon's alive,"' said Lord Selvington wearily.

'Yes!' said Blessed, crashing his fist onto the table. 'That's it! Gordon IS alive! I must find him at once. Stand back! Make way! Together we shall rid the universe of the tyrant, Ming! THUS IT MUST AND SHALL BE!' And so yelling, he charged right through the middle of the circle of tables, luckily only knocking over the two behind, where no one was sitting. As the actor passed her, yodelling in fury, Mrs Trench mumbled in her sleep and turned over, farting again.

It took a few minutes for order to be restored. The tables were put back in place, cups of tea re-poured and returned, and at last enough of a pretence of decorum returned to the meeting for Lord Selvington to invite in another candidate.

The next person to come through the door was also a man, but quite a different proposition from Brian Blessed in every way. He stood in the centre of the room with the proud gait of a matador, tall coloured feathers sprouting from his headdress, a long black cloak swathing the rest of him from head to foot. He looked gauntly down at them all, one by one, and they were each struck by the thunderous certainty of his gaze, which seemed to say, 'You know me as your superior; I see you and have the power to crush you.'

'Now, you must be Angharad,' said Selvington.

'Oh, for God's sake,' muttered the mayor.

'SPEAK NOT, WHITE MAN,' said the apparition, leaping onto a table and upsetting most of the cups of tea. 'I know your tricks! I would out-spell you with my magic. A-WOOO-YAH!' And he back-flipped off the table, getting one of his feet caught in his own gown and hitting the floor with a painful-sounding crunch.

'Ah, fuck!' said a small voice from within the swirling cloaks.

'Timmy?' said Selvington, looking up. 'Is that you?'

The cloaks were pulled back at once to reveal the furious sage, looking more over-serious than ever. 'SPEAK NOT TO ME, MAN-WHORE! I CURSE YOU TO A THOUSAND YEARS OF WALKING ON HOT BROKEN ORANGINA BOTTLES.'

'Timmy, get *up!*' said Lord Selvington, rising himself. 'This is not the place for your stupid pranks. Look, even your face paint's starting to come off. You could have broken your ankle with that jump, and then you'd miss the bloody boat race. Come on, get the hell on home with you, and I'm stopping your allowance for a month.'

'I CURSE YOU, WHITE MAN!' shouted the apparition again as it sped limping out of the door, to the relief of pretty much everyone except the Miss Quimples, who clapped excitedly. Meanwhile Mrs Trench dutifully mopped at the many cups of spilled tea.

'NEXT!' bellowed Lord Selvington.

'Ah, there you are, Dad, old chap,' said a posh young man, coming in and sitting down in the chair reserved for the interviewees. 'I was wondering if I could borrow a bit of money.' Sam immediately recognized him as the man whom he and Bradley had nearly crashed into yesterday.

'What's his name again?' asked Bradley.

'Horace. Or Sir Egbert, I think,' whispered Sam.

'For Christ's sake,' said Selvington. 'This is not the place! I've just had your idiot brother in here making an absolute bloody mockery of this meeting.'

'Oh yes, I know that. I gave him a lift up here. Thought it was rather a jolly wheeze.'

'And you thought you'd come in here afterwards and try to knock me up for some cash?'

'Well, yes, I did rather – just a couple of thousand to see me until my next book advance comes through.'

'Don't you know we're trying to replace Terry Fairbreath?'

'Oh yes, that's right. I knew there was something else. I want to be on the Parish Council too.'

'Well, you can't! Just go over there and sit in the bloody corner, will you, and we can talk about this later!'

'But what about Timmy? He'll be waiting for me in the car.'

'He can fly home with his spirit guide for all I care. NEXT!'

Horace (or Sir Egbert) came and sat next to Sam in the corner, where they said a cheery hallo to each other as the next candidate came in.

'Now *you* must be Professor Angharad Trefusis,' said Lord Selvington to the six-year-old child who came in and sat on the chair. The mayor slapped his hand against his forehead, while Sam settled in for a bit of a snooze.

Chapter Nine

'WELL, THAT WAS JOLLY, wasn't it?' said Horace as he handed Sam a cigarette. They were standing beside the door as the others made their way out behind them.

'What, the bit where your father turned down your request for money, calling you a pointless wastrel and piece of pond scum, or where the little girl wet herself during his questioning over her policies?'

'Yes, the search for Terry's replacement goes on. Hey, listen, never mind the old man. He's just cross with me because of the whole "public intellectual" thing I insist on doing, he thinks it's beneath the dignity of the family.'

'What's that, then?'

'Oh, you know – I knock out a book now and then, a novel here, bit of psychogeography there. New one's my reminiscences of doing crack with W.G. Sebald on the fens. Appear on *Newsnight* now and then, just to keep old Jozza happy.'

'Jozza?'

'Yes – you know Jozza. That chap who introduces

Newsnight. Jozza Paxo. Jeremy Oxocube. Old Pimply Paxington. My old man was at Cambridge with him, they used to gad about on the river and so forth. So I pop up on *Newsnight* from time to time to chat about this and that. Load of old rot, really, but keeps me busy between games of croquet.'

'And your proper name *is* Sir Egbert, right?'

'Ah – not any more, no.'

'Oh dear. What's happened?'

'Well, it would appear I'm now Lord Ickham of Highchurch.'

'What's this, a promotion?'

'If you want to put it that way, yes. My great-uncle passed away, on my mother's side.'

'I'm sorry to hear it.'

'Well, he was a hundred and seven.'

'Ah. So his hang-gliding days were over.'

'Oh, good Lord, yes! He had to stop that way back in March. Although, to be honest, even then it was on the orders of the local magistrate. He said, "Wear some clothes, or don't do it at all." So he chose not to do it at all.'

'He was a man of principle.'

'Well, that was Uncle Hugo all over, you see. Could never bear to back down from a position. He was that way when it came to the Nazis, and the same when it came to nude hang-gliding.'

'A staunch opponent of Hitler,' said Sam.

Lord Ickham looked awkward for a moment. 'Y-y-y-yes . . . Yes. Let's say that he was that.' He swiftly changed the subject. 'You haven't seen an ogre round here by any chance, have you?'

This made Sam's head swim for a moment as he tried to work out how to answer diplomatically. The first remark that came to mind was, 'No, but I saw Gandalf having a wazz behind the bike sheds earlier.' Instead he managed to mumble, 'Er, no, I'm pretty sure that would have stuck in my mind. Why, er . . . why do you ask?' he ventured, with some misgiving. People who abused alcohol and handed out amphetamines could be a lot of fun, but those who saw ogres tended to be acid-soaked hippies or paranoid schizophrenics, neither of whose company he found very relaxing.

Horace was frowning as he scanned the bushes and trees in the corner of the graveyard. 'Oh, no reason,' he said lightly, still glancing over his shoulder. 'Hey look, anyway – you seemed interested in some pills last time we met. Can I sort you out with anything?'

Sam looked over *his* shoulder to check that Bradley wasn't nearby. He seemed to be chatting to the vicar for the time being. 'That would be great,' he said. 'What have you got?'

'Well, now, let's not be too obvious. Come back here

behind this sarcophagus and I'll see if I can't sort you out with something . . .'

The two young men retreated to a place of greater privacy and there conducted some business with which both sides were very happy: Horace taking away the best part of a hundred pounds, and Sam pocketing eight pills and a small clear plastic envelope of white powder.

'Now, the pills are very nice indeed,' Horace was explaining. 'A very special batch.'

'I've not seen any like this before,' said Sam, holding one of the pills up to look at it. 'What is it?'

At that moment the vicar and the detective appeared around the side of the church from the opposite direction they had expected, and rather than try to make up a reason why he was standing in a graveyard buying pills from the minor aristocracy, Sam flung the tablet into his mouth. Then for no reason in particular he threw one arm behind him, leant back against the sarcophagus and affected a highly theatrical and suspicious air of nonchalance, staring with deep fascination at the new Lord Ickham, nodding and saying, 'Mm-hmm, mm-hmm,' as though agreeing with him, even though the other man wasn't saying anything at all.

'You *idiot*,' he thought to himself. 'You could easily have said that you were getting an aspirin off him, feeling like your headache might come back. There was no need to take the pill! You've never even taken these things before. How fast do they act?'

'Reverend Archie Smallcreak, meet Sam Easton. Sam's a writer.'

'How lovely to meet you,' said the little man, shaking his hand somewhat damply. 'You seem remarkably well turned out, may I say. I always understood the cliché of the young writer these days was of an alcoholic drug addict.'

'Ha-HAAAH!' yelled Sam manically. 'Steady on,' he thought. 'They haven't even kicked in yet.'

'What do you write?' enquired the vicar, smiling.

'Oh,' said Sam, sure he was making a fool of himself and determined not to say any of the titles of his awful books. 'Oh, just . . . just shit, really.'

'I see,' said Smallcreak. 'Well, if that's your game, you should try and get into the loo-book business. That *I Before E (Except After C)* book was jolly good fun – I bought six copies!'

'Jolly good,' said Sam softly, keeping his composure by replaying in his mind the scene from *The Omen* where the priest gets impaled from above by an iron spike.

'Archie was suggesting that we visit the library. Miss Elvesdon will be most happy to help us, apparently, and she's there this afternoon.'

'I'm just as concerned for Terry Fairbreath's welfare as anyone,' said the Reverend. 'He was a gentle soul, very well read and always good company. I'm still quite new here, but at the back of my mind is a lurking fear that there may have been other missing persons cases, and I was thinking you should have a look at the newspaper archives.'

'Bloody good plan,' said Sam. 'Er, sorry,' he added, and did the sign of the cross. 'Surely it can't be kicking in this quickly,' he wondered. A moment before, the young intellectual aristocrat had slipped into the shadows at the mention of drugs and so Bradley and Sam walked back to their car alone.

'*I Before E*,' said Sam spitefully. '*I Before Bollocks*, more like!'

'That's not a very nice thing to say, Sam,' said the detective complacently.

'Not at all,' said Sam, getting into the car. 'That's what my follow-up parody of *I Before E* was called. Bloody thing didn't sell a copy.'

'Oh, well. At least the Reverend liked it.'

'You're not really listening, are you?'

'I think the library's just on the left, down here . . .' said Bradley, pulling away.

Chapter Ten

THE LIBRARY WAS housed in what had once been a some-what grim-looking Victorian schoolhouse on a deserted side street. As they were standing outside waiting to be admitted, Sam noticed something strange further up the road: what looked like a hundred or so bags of rubbish by the kerb. It seemed totally out of keeping with the rest of the area. Instead of being cleared up, as he thought anything unsightly around there would surely be at pretty much a moment's notice, it had been cordoned off with roadworks signs.

They pressed the bell again and looked doubtfully up at the library building. It didn't seem as though there was anyone inside, or indeed that it had been open any time in the past twenty years, but presently Miss Elvesdon came to the door and opened it.

'I'm sorry to keep you waiting, gentlemen,' she said demurely.

Sam was about to reply that it was perfectly all right when a strange, deep rumbling sound stopped him. For a moment he thought it was his stomach, or Bradley's, and then for an even more awful one, that it was Miss Elvesdon's. But it was too deep, too loud. It seemed to come up from beneath them to shake the cobblestones.

'What—' began Bradley.

'This way, please, gentlemen,' the librarian said briskly, ushering them inside. Then she was marching them down the corridor towards her small office at the back of the building. 'Early closing today, but I stayed open for you. It's nice to have official guests,' she said. 'Or exciting for me, anyway. We mostly get the little old ladies round here. One so rarely has male company . . .'

'Is it just me,' said Bradley into Sam's ear, 'or was that the largest fart I've ever heard in my life?'

Sam refused to reply. Partly because he couldn't think of anything to say, except that he'd never felt an underground fart (or rather, an underground explosion) before, and partly because his mind was starting to race.

Seen close up, Miss Elvesdon wasn't quite so fusty as Sam had first imagined. The 'prim librarian' was clearly a look that she had cultivated on a professional basis, but behind the large glasses and deliberately unshowy hair with strands of grey, she was a slim forty-year-old, who was in conspicuously too good a shape to be a country librarian.

As he walked behind her, it began to occur to Sam that trapped as he was here in this tiny town, besides this morning's haughty waitress, this was the first female he'd seen to whom he could summon up even the mildest attraction. Added to this, he noticed that the individual candle bulbs placed along the walls were giving a slight strobing effect that was making his mind race excitedly.

'Oh no,' he thought. 'It's starting already . . . Look straight ahead. Take deep breaths. I'm horny and trapped in what looks very much like the 1930s, and I've just taken a barbiturate of unknown strength.'

Looking straight ahead, though, Sam found himself following the movement of Miss Elvesdon's hips beneath her brown wool skirt. Stop it!

'Here we are,' she said, leading them to a desk. Behind it several metal storage cabinets stood open and there were many cardboard boxes laid out on the tables, a few near the top showing that they contained old editions of the local newspaper, the *Mumford Argus and Advertiser*.

'Look at this: "Rise in teenage delinquency caused by children gorging themselves on dangerously unhealthy 'iced creams' which are being callously marketed directly at our youth." Nothing changes.'

'When was that?'

'2003.'

'Can I fetch you a drink, gentlemen?'

'Bit early for that . . .' mumbled Bradley, before meeting

her eye and saying, 'Oh, I see. Thanks. A tea would be smashing.'

A tea *would* be smashing, thought Sam. Yes. If you think about it, smashing is *exactly* what tea is. That's a pretty profound thing to . . . 'Sorry,' he said. 'My mind was wandering. Did it take me embarrassingly ages to respond?'

Miss Elvesdon said nothing, and Bradley dropped the paper he was reading and turned to look at him.

'Hmm,' said Sam. 'Tea, please, thanks. And tortoise milk. No! Milk! Just ordinary milk.'

'No sugar?'

'No, I'm not a monster,' he said absently, before being swamped once more by his own thoughts.

'So, old Archie Smallcreak thought there might be evidence here of past crimes. I'll take 1972–74, you have this box, 1983–85. Look through for anything suspicious.'

'You mean like murders?' Sam said dully.

'Yes, Sam, well done. Exactly like murders.'

'She's so sexy.'

'*What?*'

'Nothing. I didn't say anything.'

Miss Elvesdon returned with the tea in due course and left the men to their study, promising to return if they wanted anything before she locked up at six.

Peace descended as Bradley methodically worked his way through the newspapers in front of him and Sam scrabbled furiously through his between becoming obsessed with particular pieces or adverts for minutes on end.

'Here, look at this . . .' Bradley said. 'Terrible murder case. Man found mutilated on the moors.'

'I didn't know there were any moors round here,' said Sam.

'Shush! Listen, he was found with "Thou shalt not commit adultery" carved into his back. And his *brain* was taken out. God, look at this, too – the very next day another body was found. And this had "Thou shalt not steal" carved on it.'

'Here,' said Sam, skipping ahead a few weeks. 'Apparently he did all ten. That seems a bit strong for all of them, doesn't it? Isn't one of them just about honouring the Sabbath? Oh, and look – they got him. "Commandments Killer Caught – the man they labelled Cecil B. DeKILL was captured yesterday, blah blah blah."'

'Hmm,' said Bradley, disappointed.

'But wait a minute, what's this? Look, in the 1966 file. Man found decapitated in the woods. Then,' he flipped over the next newspaper, 'next day, a woman's body discovered. His name is Jack, her surname is Queen. Then the next day, look – a man named King is found disembowelled.'

'They've dubbed him the Playing Card Killer,' said Bradley, coming over and taking the paper. 'Maybe we're on to something!'

'Yes, but then I suppose there's not a card in the conventional pack called the Fairbreath. Or the Terry. And it happened forty-six years ago. Do serial murderers often leave a gap that large?'

'Maybe his middle name's Ace,' said Bradley, searching through the old newspapers.

'No, here we are,' said Sam. '"Lauren Ace, respected publicist for a well-known British publisher, was spared the attentions of the Playing Card Killer as the murderer was caught hours before he had a chance to make his move."'

'So they got him,' said Bradley, crestfallen.

Some minutes passed before he spoke up again. 'Look *here!*' he said. 'March 1972. Apparently there was a sudden huge attack of telekinesis. Poltergeists destroyed homes, ghouls swarmed through the streets and covered the place with green ectoplasm; the dead rose from their graves.'

'Good Lord!'

'But apparently four guys turned up in a station wagon and sorted it out lickety-split. Then the *following* year there was a local rollercoaster that was supposedly haunted, but this time four kids with a cowardly Great Dane turned up in a van to investigate, and it turned out that it wasn't haunted at all, it had just been the guy who was running the rollercoaster all along, wearing a mask.'

'Gosh,' said Bradley. 'I bet he was really ticked off to be caught out by a bunch of meddling kids!'

'It's insane. This place seems to be some sort of nexus for terrible crimes, but they've all been solved!'

'Can I help you two gentlemen?' said Miss Elvesdon from the doorway.

'Yes, please,' said Bradley. 'The Reverend seemed to think there was something for us here, perhaps in the reports of old crimes. But we've been through everything and there doesn't seem to be a clue as to anything that Terry Fairbreath would have been interested in.'

Was Sam imagining it, or was Miss Elvesdon leaning somewhat coquettishly against the door? And the way she waggled that pencil and then occasionally looked at him with the pretence of disinterest. Surely she was being deliberately provocative. God, he really had to stop grinding his teeth . . .

'It's certainly true that Terry had come to see me,' said Miss Elvesdon, 'and he looked through these files just the same as you did, but he seemed to go away disappointed. I never knew what he was looking for – except . . .'

'Except?' asked Sam. Accept *me*! Let's go to the— Stop it!

'Except he made some cryptic remark about the Hill, which I didn't understand. I didn't want to interrupt him at the time because he seemed to be in a world of his own, but I wondered what he meant.'

'We're surrounded by hills. Which hill?'

'Ah – here in town when we say the Hill, we mean the one that rises behind the abbey.'

'We went up there,' said Bradley. 'Infested with hippies.'

'Are they really hippies? I'm not so sure. The townsfolk always seem quite scared of them, and don't speak about them the way I would expect well-off posh folk to dismiss crusties like that. That Hill is something that people – older people – don't talk about. They always change the conversation when you bring it up, and I don't understand entirely why.'

'These newspapers only go back to the late 1950s. Do you think there could be another earlier record?'

'Oh, yes – I never had a chance to tell Mr Fairbreath about it, he left before I could speak to him. But I was told that when the library moved in here, the pre- and immediately post-war collections were housed in the basement of the abbey. You might find something there.'

'Thank you, Mrs Elvesdon,' said Bradley. 'You've been most obliging. May I use your facilities?'

'Just down there,' she said, pointing him the way, before turning back to face Sam. 'And it's *Miss*,' she said, coming to sit near him. She perched on the edge of the table next to his chair so that she was above him. His body temperature rose by about nine degrees.

'Tell me, Mr Easton,' she said. 'What is it that you write?'

'Nothing,' he said emphatically. Then he blinked. 'Nothing you would have heard of, I daresay.' Then he struggled to clear his throat for several seconds.

'Oh, you never know. I might look like a quiet little librarian, but I'm very broad-minded . . .'

'I think I know where she's going with this,' he thought. His blood pressure continued to rocket.

'My personal interest is in erotic fiction,' she said.

'Oh God!'

'I'd be delighted to show you my collection, if you ever wanted to see . . .'

That was it. She had said it – made a direct invitation.

Sam had by now very certainly cruised far beyond and above any legal, medical or psychological definition of the phrase 'being high'. His mind raced, and he could only respond to her advances by avoiding her gaze and bobbing his head forwards and backwards to an imagined beat. There were two things at that moment (with the certainty of the stoner) that he knew to be absolutely true. One of them was that this somewhat attractive woman was trying to have sex with him. And the other was that his upbringing made it almost literally impossible for this to happen.

'Any time,' she said, placing her hand on his leg. He gazed at her. 'You see, while I like to read about it, I don't get much chance to put the theory into practice . . .' The blood was now pumping so fast around Sam's veins that some of it was starting to overlap.

'Yuh,' he said. 'Ahem. Yeehuh, I, uh, I – oh, there you are, Bradley. Miss Elvesdon was just helping me with my, er, leg.'

'Oh good. Is it feeling better? Come on, we'd better get on up to the Abbey. It's nearly dark and I don't want to be skulking around there all night.'

'You never know who you might meet,' said the librarian, running a finger down Sam's spine, out of the sight of Bradley.

'Coming,' said Sam.

Chapter Eleven

'THE OLD ARCHIVES?' asked Archie Smallcreak, standing in his own doorway wearing carpet slippers, and as friendly as ever. 'I'd forgotten they were ever put in there. But she's quite right. Let me fetch the key.' As he bustled away up the stairs, Bradley turned a suspicious eye to Sam.

'You all right?' he asked.

'I'm fine,' whispered Sam, his eyes wide. 'Quite fine.'

'That hangover's really caught up with you, hasn't it?'

'Tell the truth,' said Sam, struggling to get the words out, 'the hair of the dog would probably do me a bit of good, yes.' This was, however, a distant prospect as before them stretched a potentially lengthy, chilly and pointless search for information based on a half-formed hunch. And just as the phrase 'half-formed hunch' popped into his mind, Sam was disturbed once more by the sight of Mrs Trench pushing a squeaking mop lugubriously around the vicar's porch. She stopped and raised her head very slowly to take them in, regarded them for a few seconds, then lowered it again and moved on.

'It's like meeting glances with a berthing whale,' muttered Sam.

'She's certainly no oil painting, I'll give you that,' said Bradley.

'There we are,' said Archie, reappearing not with one or two keys, but what appeared to be the medieval gaoler's stock-in-trade: a gargantuan cast-iron ring, from which hung perhaps three dozen rust-toothed keys. 'Better follow me closely, it gets a bit dark round the back here . . .'

As the Reverend stepped into the beautifully-kept garden, Bradley followed him, whistling, but Sam had a sudden and very morbid presentiment. It was as though someone had walked over his grave, he thought to himself. Either that, or the idea of climbing down into a thousand-year-old sepulchre accompanied by PC Plod's less intelligent cousin from the country, while on drugs, gave him the willies.

As they walked, Smallcreak explained the great building's history. The abbey, it seemed, was relatively famous – although Sam wondered whether *most* abbeys probably were, he didn't think there were that many of them around. This one had been the subject of a high-profile charity drive to save it from collapsing in the late 1980s, when several million had been raised to have the foundations replaced. When this work was being carried out, however, the windows had been found to be in too poor a shape for it to be reopened, and a further and more protracted effort was mounted to raise the necessary funds to have the stained glass touched up and largely replaced. Then, before it had opened again, squatters had moved in, and only vacated the place five years later when they were offered much more comfortable council housing in nearby Fraxbridge. Then the roof had needed to be repaired, which meant that all in all, a congregation hadn't seen the inside since shortly after Sam's second birthday. It was a tall and magnificent edifice, even seen here from the back, and rose over them menacingly as they descended through the shadows to the crypt door.

'Fascinating,' said Bradley, looking up at it. 'Tell me, does it date from the same era as that lovely house on the top of the hill, where the er, famous auth—'

'Oh, good Lord, me!' said the vicar, swinging the keys round his wrist so that they jangled horribly, then throwing them clean over his shoulder. 'Oh dear!' he shouted over his shoulder as he scampered to pick them up. 'I must stop doing that!'

Sam was deeply freaked out by this behaviour, but Bradley showed no surprise at all as the little man beetled back towards them, jangling the keys louder than ever, and he said equably, 'I was asking if that large house—'

'Oh, dearie me! The jangling of the keys is so loud I can't hear you!' shouted the vicar, with manic eyes.

'Please, please make it stop,' said Sam quietly, and in some confusion Bradley desisted his questioning. The keys became quiet.

'Here we go, then! Let's get cracking!' said Smallcreak cheerfully, darting to the door and trying the keys, one by one, until the lock clicked open.

'What was that about?' whispered Bradley.

'I don't know,' said Sam. 'Just ask him never to do that again. I think he might have broken one of my ears with all that jangling!'

The stone door made a long, attenuated whining noise as it swung inwards, disclosing no more than a pit of darkness within.

'Light switch?' asked Sam weakly.

'What am I thinking? Of course, it'll be terribly dark in there – I'll fetch a candle.'

Even Bradley seemed momentarily daunted when the Reverend returned and, stepping inside, they found that they could only see a few feet ahead of themselves. Beyond the wet stone flags, darkness swallowed up the flickering candlelight.

'Perhaps you'd better go first,' said Bradley.

'Oh yes, I suppose that is sensible. Mind how you go, gentlemen.' The noise of his voice echoed down the dark chamber and came back up to them, joined by others (or so it seemed to Sam, over the noise of his fast-beating heart).

Scratching, perhaps of claws, what might be distant foot-steps, and a whispery breeze that if he listened to it closely he was sure would resolve itself into a voice – he stuffed his fingers into his ears and hummed gently to make sure this couldn't happen.

'I wonder what would happen if I shat myself,' thought Sam. Which then made him think – 'I'd probably be allowed to go home. But go home *where*? I haven't checked into a bed and breakfast yet!'

'Bugger it!' he muttered.

'What was that?' asked Bradley.

They had now descended far enough for what light that had been coming from above to be completely invisible, and Sam leant forward to be included in the candle's glare, like someone leaning hopelessly to get in under an umbrella.

When Archie spoke again, his voice took on another note entirely. It was low, creeping, afraid, as it said: 'There are strange things in this place.' Bradley and Sam exchanged a look. 'Dark and dangerous things,' Archie went on. 'Things man should never even *dream* of!'

A beep went off in his pocket, making the other two jump.

'Oh look, the Bishop's retweeted my remark about the Dead Sea Scrolls! Let me just quote-tweet. Which button is it? Ah . . . "Ha! U so right, @Bishthedish! Dead sea scrolls

#debatable #whowrotethem c u soon you big dishpot! MEGALOLZ! ;P".'

The other two men waited uncomfortably on the cramped spiral staircase as the Reverend tapped the message out with his thumb.

'You were saying about dark things . . .' prompted Sam.

'Oh, yes,' he said, pocketing his iPhone and at once resuming his former manner. 'Dark. Dark! Dark, indeed!' Turning back, he hollered melodramatically into their faces, pulling a twisted expression indicative of deep horror. 'I'm rehearsing my speech for the Christmas play we're putting on. It's *The Pit and the Pendulum*. What do you think?'

'On balance, I suppose I'd rather you were doing *The Sound of Music*,' said Sam.

'We did that last year. Word of advice – never use live ammunition in a stage musical. It was a legal nightmare . . .'

'I don't understand. There aren't any gunshots in *The Sound of Music*, are there?'

'I don't recall the original movie, but by the time Judge Barnstable had got through with the script it was an absolute bloodbath . . .' His voice faded as he reached the bottom of the steps.

'Right. Here's the crypt, then. Old archive is right there at the back, behind the stage sets for *Young Frankenstein*, which was the play we did a few years back at the insistence of the old German doctor, who used to live hereabouts. No longer with us, though – terrible business.' So saying, Smallcreak lit a second candle he produced from his pocket, handed it over to Bradley and with a rapid 'Toodle-pip, then, lads!' scampered back up the stairs before they could think of a pretext to keep him with them.

'Okay, so . . .' said Bradley, inching forward.

Behind him, with the pill now in full force, Sam had taken to bobbing his head and moving his shoulders in rhythmic fashion, all the while staring left and right in a perfect transport of terror.

'You, er . . . You frightened at all back there, Sam?'

There was a little rattle of a stone tumbling from the wall and rocking onto the floor.

'Slightly,' said Sam. 'A bit, yes. You?'

'I remember when I had to go in first place at the head of an armed unit when we broke into a sixth-floor apartment. It was dark and gloomy, and there were hundreds of those car-smell things hanging from the ceiling, and we discovered a body stretched out on the bed. It had all the flesh scraped from its face, even its eyelids were cut off. And when we got up close . . . we found that it was *still alive*,' said Bradley. 'That was less scary than this.'

'I think you're thinking of the film *Se7en*, Detective,' said Sam.

'Am I? Oh yes, so I am. Well, it was still less scary than this, though.'

As this conversation progressed both men started to talk more and more quietly, until they were almost inaudible to each other. The reason for this was that there were now definite and unmistakeable sounds coming from either side of them. There was a rustle of fabric, and then a noise that sounded like a muffled cough.

'It could just be the wind,' whispered Bradley.

'Yes,' said Sam, his senses so inflamed that he could now practically see through time. 'It could also be the beast from seven fathoms that we have disturbed in its lair, salivating at the prospect of tearing us to pieces with its tentacles and sucking out our insides in a single gurgling slurp.'

'You're not helping,' whispered Bradley.

Into the weak, wavering circle of light there now came some shapes. There seemed to be a raised tomb, and on top of it a supine form, and . . . could it be . . . on top of that a light like a phantom eye, burning angry orange, growing wider?

'Argh! Bloody hell!' yelled Bradley.

'They're coming for us!' said Sam, turning to run and seeing two human forms before him, hooded, their faces wearing nasty grins and lit up by an unearthly glow.

Bradley stumbled in the opposite direction, through the set of *Young Frankenstein*, then bumped into a wall, where he felt a light switch and turned it on.

Sam found himself standing in front of two teenagers in

hoodies, a boy and a girl, who weren't wearing horrible grins at all, but were clearly terrified.

'Who the fuck are you?' he asked.

'I'm Beatrix,' said one. 'And he's Rupert.'

The lighting flickered on in about six different bulbs around them, and revealed this underground chamber to be not quite the location of *The Tomb of Ligeia*, as Sam had feared, but nothing more than rubble-strewn bunker, with arched alcoves leading off to the sides, filled with all kinds of leftover building materials and forgotten storage junk.

'And he's Piers,' said Rupert, pointing to a third teen, who was standing behind what looked in the dark like a raised tomb but was in fact a rather unconvincing and plas-ticky dissection table – belonging, no doubt, to the fictional Dr Frankenstein.

'Hullo,' said Piers, who was smoking a particularly long joint. This had been the orange eye that had seemed sud-denly to flare open in the dark.

'Oh, my God!' said Sam, letting out a deep breath and sitting down on a coffin that was leaning on its side. Bradley was more embarrassed by the idea that he might have appeared afraid in front of such youths, and after blowing out the candle, he immediately set to work searching through the filing cabinets, trying to locate which of them contained the newspaper archive.

'What are you guys *doing* down here?' asked Sam.

'Taking drugs,' shrugged Beatrix. 'What does it look like?'

'Hey, well, listen – can I have a bit of that? You scared the flippin' life out of me. Cheers. Oh, that's good. Listen, don't let that guy over there see, he's a policeman, but would you, er – would you have any spare that I could buy?'

The teenagers looked shyly at each other and went into some sort of conclave for a few moments before conceding they could spare him ten pounds' worth, and saying if he came to Hotspots, the nightclub, he'd be able to buy more from Gavin, their dealer.

'This'll do me for now. Damn, I'm grateful!' he said, as the cannabis soothingly refined the nasty teeth-grinding, heart-squeezing edge from the mystery pill he had taken.

'If you're not a policeman, why you hanging around wit one?'

'I've seen *The Wire* too, Rupert, and that accent's not convincing, I'm afraid. I'm a writer.'

'Oh yeah?' said Piers. 'Have you written anything I might have read?'

'Do you read books?'

'Not really.'

'Well, then, it's quite unlikely – no, wait, actually you're exactly the sort of person who might have read one. Ever read those stupid books you find in other people's toilets?'

'The funny ones? Yeah, I read them when I take a dump.'

'Well, there's my science trivia parody, *Don't Fuck a Whale in the Spout*. You're best off not reading that one, it's basically comedy animal porn. I did ghostwrite the *Angina Monologues* by Ken Clarke. Er, what else? How about my literary erotica – *The Curious Incident of the Dogging in the Night Time*? But I'm getting off the point. Hey, you guys've got cider! I'll give you twice its street value . . .'

Sam was now very high, not really making sense, talking much faster than he should and into the bargain, handing over a ludicrous amount of money for the two-litre bottle of cider that Beatrix happily parted with.

'So why are you kids in the freezing cold down here? Why aren't you in one of the local parks?'

'You're kidding, aren't you?' said Piers.

'Why would I be kidding?'

'Those "gardens", as they're known, win prizes for the best in England. They're patrolled by the granny mafia. You don't mess with the mafia,' he said, looking deadly serious.

'Oh,' smiled Sam. 'I see. Wait a second, did you just say there's a nightclub in this godforsaken place? Called Hotspots?'

They told him indeed there was, and gave him directions on how to find it. It seemed there were a few backstreets tucked away behind the town's picture-perfect square, where one more used to city life might find some of the amenities to which he was more used.

'A fried chicken shop? I'll bet it's not called Tennessee Fried Chicken or Kansas Fried Chicken, like they are back in London.'

'You're right. Ye Olde Fried Chicken. Next to the taxi place.'

'A kebab shop?'

'The Eye of Constantinople, just over from the betting shop.'

'Ye Olde Betting Shoppe?'

'You got it.'

'And an Indian?'

'The Jewel of the Empire.'

'This gets better and better. Thanks, guys!' And waving them off with sincere hopes that they might see each other at Hotspots later (he was hardly likely to sleep, after all), Sam turned back to join the detective.

'How's it going?' he asked.

'Those lads gone?' said Bradley. 'What were they doing down here?'

'Oh,' said Sam vaguely, 'research for a history project, I think. What have you found?'

'Well, more crimes, that's for certain. This place is insane. Look at this: 1958, thirty people massacred on top of the Hill.'

'Hill with a capital H?'

'That's the one. Massive manhunt across the whole

country – turns out it was a suicide pact by a cult based around the Egyptian God Osiris.'

'Shame they had to take everything so Osiris-ly!' said Sam jubilantly, well pleased with his efforts. Bradley did not respond at first, too engrossed in the newspaper, and then looked over his shoulder down the dusty chamber in which they were standing.

'They could have worshipped down here, for all we know,' he said, turning back to his paper. Sam kept looking after him, bringing the booze out of his pocket and taking a nervous swig.

'Then there's this: 1956. Man found torn to shreds in the woods, from apparent wolf attack. Closer inspection shows he was murdered. Then two weeks later, another body found with bite marks on neck, apparently victim of a vampire attack. Murders connected by relation to the monsters in the old Universal horror movies.'

Sam looked up at the sets for *Young Frankenstein* and shivered.

'But *again*, look here. Murderer caught. It was the local projectionist, objecting to Hammer Horror's plans to remake the old Universal classics.'

'He was quite right,' said Sam. 'The Hammer monster pictures were far inferior but some of their other movies were great. Have you ever seen *Taste of Fear*? Or *Quatermass and the Pit*? They're bloody marvellous!'

'That's not the *point*, is it, Sam? The key point is, there are no loose ends in these cases! So we've still no idea what Terry was looking for in the newspaper archive.'

Sam sat and took a pile of papers that hadn't been examined yet and started flicking through. After the unpleasant shocks of the last half-hour it proved a pleasant way to slowly calm down. Getting into the rhythm of the pages spinning in front of his eyes, he scanned and turned them quickly, progressing with more speed than he could have hoped through the years 1953, 1952, 1951 . . . At one point he absent-mindedly rolled himself a joint and, having lit it, offered it to Bradley before realizing what he was doing. But the detective in his cloistered village upbringing didn't seem to have ever come across marijuana before because he simply shook his head, and carried on reading.

Like anyone who has to rapidly skim through research, after scanning perhaps two thousand pages Sam was beginning to wonder whether he was really taking anything in at all, and whether he might have long ago missed an incredibly obvious clue, such as a headline like 'UNSOLVED MURDER IN CASE NOT LIKELY TO BE SOLVED FOR THE NEXT FIFTY YEARS – UNTIL THE YEAR 2012, SAY'. But at last he came across something that stirred in his mind.

'What does this mean?' he asked. 'This local character, whatever he's called, McElwee, is deemed to be a suspicious bloke owing to "his behaviour in relation to the controversial recent matter of the local Hill". Hill with a capital H once more.'

'I wonder what that means.'

'But this McElwee character seems to have been imprisoned for no crime at all, just for sniffing around the Hill. Here, have half my stack, it's obviously in this pile somewhere.'

No sooner had Sam passed him a handful of papers than Bradley found something decidedly suspicious. He held up for Sam's inspection the letters page of a copy of the *Mumford Argus* (as it had then been), with four of the seven letters cut out of it. The sight sent a chill down Sam's spine, where one can only assume it jostled in among the half-dozen other chills that had been travelling up and down his spine under various circumstances all day.

'There's another comment here – "Mrs Waldicott's testimony as a witness is certainly damning, if it can be believed. However, it cannot be forgotten she was a notorious protestor in the recent matter of the otherwise universally approved scheme with regard to our great Hill." Weird! What the hell are they talking about?'

Sam and Bradley worked together for another hour, searching the archive of the early 1950s for further references to this mystery. When they had concluded, they laid out the evidence and Bradley made note of it while Sam paced back and forth and narrated.

'We've got no fewer than fifty-four articles cut out or partially excised from the paper after June 1951. Most of the big ones are in those few months, June to September. After that it peters out. Now we've got no evidence to back this up, but—'

Bradley looked up from his pad. 'But there's circumstantial evid—'

'Objection OVERRULED! *My* witness! Let me finish.'

'I think you've had too much of that vodka. Can you stop waving the bottle aro—'

'Objection overruled! Will the Counsel please let me finish. Okay – okay, I'll be more careful with the bottle. I did get you that time, sorry. Our conjecture, your Honour – *Ladies and Gentlemen of the Jury* – is that something happened to do with that hill in the summer of 1951. Something controversial. And the persons who claimed that it wasn't a good idea were victimized.'

'Stop talking to the bloody wall, Sam! Talk to me. I just want to get this straight. We think that people who objected to this scheme, whatever it was, were victimized in some way; made to feel like outcasts. Then there are these six isolated and mysterious references in other articles to people who are called things like "notorious troublemaker" and "objector to the beneficial scheme". And we think these are the ones that slipped through because the other pieces which have been cut out are also references to the same thing.'

'Exactly. And those who didn't up sticks and move away were victimized even further.'

'Because,' said Bradley, going back to a newspaper he had placed on the floor and holding it up, 'it seems all these monstrous crimes that happened throughout the following years were perpetrated upon the very same people who objected in the first place. The six names we have all match: Waldicott, Tennyson, Hibblewick, Tavistock, Jerome, Duffield. All brutally murdered.'

'God damn it, I love it when we crack a case like this!' said Sam.

'I really think you should put the vodka down. And stop smoking that terrible skunk, or whatever it is.'

'Oh, I thought you didn't know what it was.'

'Of course I do. I've got a television set, haven't I? I don't care a crumb what you smoke, I've got bigger fish to fry. Come on, I'm starving. Let's get a meal here in town and then drive back to Fraxbridge.'

Chapter Twelve

During the drive back to the centre of town, Sam, who was temporarily on another high after their detective work, lobbied successfully, by a process of whining until Bradley could take no more, for them to eat their meal in the pub rather than a local restaurant. By the time they arrived in the car park he had slumped again into a semi-torpid and introspective state, and had embarked on the tediously contemplative stage of being high.

'You know Raffles, the gentleman thief?' he asked as they got out of the car. 'Do you reckon he was called Raffles because it rhymes with "snaffles"? Because that's sort of a posh word for steals? So the author – was it E. W. Hornung? – hoped the tagline would be "Raffles snaffles"?' He trotted along, struggling to keep up with the detective as they crossed the car park towards the pub's back door.

'Am I talking crap?' asked Sam.

'Yes.'

As they reached the doorway they heard a wolf whistle that made them turn.

Both looked left and right, mystified, and were about to continue on their way when they heard a second, more aggressive whistle and, peering through the gloom, saw that it came from a tiny figure in a battered old VW Golf about a dozen yards away. Approaching not with concern, perhaps, but certainly with confusion, they saw first that in the driver's seat was a little old lady of at least seventy-five, and second that she was languorously smoking a silver Silk Cut, with her hand lolling out of the window.

'That your car, is it, love?' she said. She was chewing gum as she spoke, and looking the other way.

'I beg your pardon?' said Bradley.

'I said, is that your car, sweetheart?' She flicked the cigarette butt so it spun in the air and bounced off the windscreen of a smart-looking Audi, ten feet away.

'Er, no . . . actually . . . That's mine, over there,' said Bradley, pointing with his little finger. 'The Prius. It's a, er, a hybrid. They're quite good . . .'

He tailed off. The old lady chewed her gum, rolled her head.

'. . . Good for that sort of thing . . . Prius . . . Can I . . . Do you need any help?'

'Oh, I don't need any help, love,' said the old lady, lasciviously looking him up and down, then lighting another Silk Cut and blowing the smoke towards him. She tilted the mirror down (quite sharply down) and checked her reflection in it. 'I got my golf clubs in the boot, and my sisters are backing me up. Reckon I'm all right.'

'Your sisters . . .' said Bradley.

The two men looked up and squinted in the darkness, and saw four separate sets of headlights blink on and off in a quick signal, one from each corner of the car park.

'Yes, I reckon I'm all right, heartface. But are *you* all right? Maybe you want to watch yourself round here.'

Bradley and Sam exchanged a look, and the detective was about to speak when the VW's engine sparked to life and the cigarette landed at his feet.

'Just thinking of your safety, boys.' She smeared a crimson lipstick across her lower lip with all the sensuality of someone hoovering a duvet, then squeezed her mouth into a pout, rubbing her lips back and forth, and leered at him. 'You look after yourself, you hear me, honey? Wouldn't want anything bad to happen to you.'

She pushed the car into gear and as it crept forward she leant out of the window and said, almost too low to hear, 'Folks round here don't like people who stick their noses in where it isn't wanted.' And before they could think how to respond, the car crawled out of the car park and pulled into the street at about twelve miles an hour. An oncoming vehicle had to break sharply and honked its horn, but she sailed off, slow as she pleased.

One after the other, the remaining cars departed as part

of the same convoy, leaving only half-smoked Silk Cuts smouldering on the gravel behind them.

'The granny mafia,' said Sam wonderingly.

'Let's get out of here,' said Bradley.

He refused to engage Sam in conversation about what had happened until they had ordered their food (Sam corrected Bradley's order of a risotto to one of burger, onion rings and chips) and sat down with their drinks in the far corner, as far from anyone else as they could be. Bradley was so confused by what had just happened, he did not demur as Sam ordered them two pints and two whisky chasers 'to save time'.

'Let's deal with that later. This case is getting exciting. I'm very pleased with our work today,' he confided. 'For a couple of non-detectives we're doing pretty well.'

'This is all terribly exciting,' said Sam. 'Am I technically deputized yet?'

'I'm not sure that's really a process that can happen in the UK. Or anywhere in the last hundred years. I feel we're closing in, but I'm not sure on what. In this situation, what would Brautigan do?'

'You really want to be like him?' asked Sam.

'God, yes,' said Bradley. 'Mrs Detective would certainly like it if I were more like him.'

'Hell *yes*, she would!' said Sam, nodding in a rather suggestive way that Bradley chose to ignore.

'More decisive.'

'Is that decisive with a question mark?'

'No,' said Bradley.

'Well, say it more decisively, then. There's no word that deserves it more. Mrs Detective would like it if you were what, big dick?' He was needling Bradley now, he could see. Making him uncomfortable.

'More de*cis*ive.'

'More derisive? She deride you?'

'No! Don't be silly. More decisive!'

'Who decides how decisive you are?' asked Sam loudly.

'I do,' said Bradley, looking away. '*I* do!' he said, looking back, annoyed with himself.

'So you're going to be more decisive, and . . . ?'

'More assertive! Good Lord, yes, I am!' Bradley was still coming across like someone who had accidentally got into a conversation by being overheard, and was desperate to slink away. Neither particularly decisive, nor assertive.

'Not "Good Lord", Detective, "God damn it".'

Bradley looked somewhat shyly back at him, as though to say: that's all right for you, but I can't carry it off.

'God DAMN it, I said!' bellowed Sam, so loud that anyone who might have been within earshot would undoubtedly stare at them. The possibility someone could be passing nearby, from the kitchens or to the toilet, still embarrassed Bradley so much he went red hot to the ears.

'*God damn it*, then,' he said quietly, but with intensity.

'Your career is on the line and it's hanging from the line by a thread. Nothing matters to you except cracking this case. You're not going to blow it, this is all you've got. You'd rather die.'

Bradley thought about that, and realized it was true.

'Then God damn it, you punk-ass motherfucker, you're not going to take any shit from anyone, are you?'

'Well . . .' said Bradley, 'certainly one of the things that's essential to good policing is calming down a potentially difficult situ—'

'I'm not talking about good policing, you pathetic punk . . .'

'Hey . . .'

'I'm talking about being a good goddam detective. Do you care about the rules?'

'Of course. What else *are* the police if you—'

'No, you don't! You're going to get your man, no matter what, and when the dust has settled they'll see that they need you more than you need them. No matter what those pen-pushers at the Town Hall squeal about down the phone. *That's* being a detective, Detective.'

'Hmm. I have to admit, it does sound good,' said Bradley, tasting his whisky.

'Hey, you know, if we run into that old bag again—'

'That's a little rude, don't you think?'

'*I'll* tell you what's rude. That granny gangster has got no respect for the *law*. She's trying to run this town in a climate of fear. Those teens I met up at the castle, the big church, the – what is it, the abbey? They're skulking around up there because they're afraid of that nasty little pensioner scum. So if she tries some of the same shit on you again,' said Sam, 'you know what you should say to her?'

'No,' said Bradley.

Sam counted the acceptable responses off on his fingers. Forefinger. 'Don't give me that shit! Repeat after me.'

'Don't give me any of that shit!' he said.

Middle finger. 'I ain't taking no for an answer, God damn it!'

'I ain't taking no for an answer, God damn it!' said Bradley.

'Still too quiet. At best you're doing a Clint Eastwood drawl. I want to see Al Pacino losing his shit. A full-on tantrum. You know, "Attica, Attica!"'

'I don't know that reference.'

'Well, it's a very rousing speech he delivers in *Dog Day Afternoon*. Where he plays, er . . . Well, he plays a gay kidnapper holding up a bank to pay for his boyfriend's sex change. So that's maybe not the best example. Imagine him as Serpico but, you know, more loud.'

Bradley fixed him with a baffled look.

'Okay, next line.' Ring finger. 'So help me, if you don't spill, I'll run your ass down to the bullpen.'

'The *bullpen*?'

'Yeah, the fuckin' bullpen! You playing innocent with me? The bullpen . . . The squad room . . . The station house . . .'

Between them they were now making so much noise that any minute they would surely attract attention from the other diners (or, possibly, other members of the local police force), so, hoping this might be the conclusion of the lesson, Bradley stood up, throwing his chair back onto the floor, and pointed right into the middle of Sam's face. 'So help me, I will run your arse right down to the police station!'

'Woa, that's good! That's good, man, sit down.'

'Can I help you, gentlemen?' called the landlord from the bar. Giving Bradley an encouraging smile, Sam got up and skipped over. He had already dealt with two whiskies and more than half his pint, so he ordered the same round all over again and asked for it to be put on Bradley's tab.

'You gentlemen, er, actors or something?' asked the landlord, with his genial skill for starting conversations intended to go nowhere.

'We're detectives!' said Sam, still addled. 'And we're going to blow this shit wide open. Just me, my boss over there and a wise-crackin' hamster!'

'Right you are,' said the landlord, placing the drinks on a tray.

'The hamster isn't here right now,' added Sam.

'You're not from round these parts, are you?' said the landlord.

'That guy's got no sense of humour,' said Sam, sitting back down. 'But I admit I am starting to feel slightly conspicuous. Where were we?'

The food arrived and they had to make room for it on their table, which involved the loud and awkward removal of several glasses and lots of splashing of still-full drinks. When they had settled into their meal, it seemed that the detective's interest had firmly been piqued, for he asked: 'What else do I need to do to be this proper detective you talk about, then?'

'You've got to swear all the time, and have no sensitivity at all for good manners.'

'Okay, good point. Thank you.'

'Hmm,' said Sam, chewing on a bit of scampi. 'And don't order the bloody risotto. What's wrong with you? It's burgers for you now, my friend – for breakfast, lunch and dinner.'

'Oh dear. I don't think that would . . .' Then he caught Sam's eye and stopped. 'What else?' he asked.

'Well, how do you get on with your wife, for instance?'

'Oh, well enough,' Bradley replied, looking slightly defeated.

'You shouldn't. You should sleep around relentlessly, never tell your wife where you are and needlessly provoke arguments with her, just to remind her that she needs you.' A reluctant glint of interest entered Bradley's eye, and Sam added: 'Of course, she'd still love you, but you'd be so difficult that she'd leave you and set up with some other, more clean-cut guy, who's less of a macho dude than you. An architect or a dentist, or something.'

'That sounds like the best of both worlds. Why would she leave me, exactly?'

'Because you'd be an alcoholic.'

With apparent insouciance, as though it had nothing to do with what Sam had just said and without finishing his mouthful of food, Bradley took an unfeasibly large gulp from his nearest pint and spilt splashes of it down either side of his chin. Then he coughed and had to hold a hand over his mouth to prevent himself from throwing up.

Watching him, Sam felt queasy to realize he had the insider knowledge that a true alcoholic would not be so reckless as to spill any of his drink. He swiftly downed a whisky to quell the thought.

'You could be a drug addict too,' he went on, 'but alcoholic will probably cover it. Along with the booze and the stress, you'd eventually get depression as well. Sorry.'

Bradley didn't seem to be completely won over by this suggestion, but manfully continued to plough through his several remaining drinks.

'There's a good chance you'll also get shot in the line of duty,' said Sam. 'But on the bright side, you'll almost certainly survive, and what's more have a rather sexy scar or limp to go with the story.'

'I'm still not completely convinced,' said Bradley, giving the younger man a sceptical look. 'I think a lot of what you're saying might be hyperbollocks.'

'No, you haven't – you don't understand that word . . .'

'I mean, you wonder why anyone wants to be a detective at all, don't you?'

'Less of that. You're earthy, but soulful,' said Sam. 'If you are prone to introspection of any kind, it would be expressed with inarticulate rage.'

Bradley chewed his food and looked depressed.

'There you go,' said Sam. 'You're getting it just right. There's one final thing, but it's the most important of all.'

'Okay,' said the detective, putting down his knife and fork, and listening as intently and hopelessly as a student at his first lesson in a foreign language.

'Above all, you *always* go with your hunch, understand? You have an intuition that's often not supported by the evidence and you're going to follow it no matter what, even if it means going against all suggestions from other people. That is what makes a great fictional detective.'

'Maybe that's enough for me to remember just now,' said Bradley, finishing yet another pint and wiping his mouth with his sleeve. His eyes were starting to swim. 'Let's talk about it later.'

'Would you like to see the dessert menu, gentlemen?' asked a barmaid.

'God damn it, I'm not taking no for an answer!' hollered Bradley, pointing at her.

'I think we should leave,' said Sam.

Chapter Thirteen

'WHERE THE FUCK'S my car?' said Bradley as they came back out into the car park.

'It doesn't really matter,' said Sam. 'You're not driving anywhere.'

'I can drive. I can drive anywhere,' slurred Bradley.

'Of course you can't. You can't even stand up straight.'

'Fuck *you*!'

'That's my boy. Come on, I'll call a cab. I need to get back to Fraxbridge soon if I'm going to find anywhere to stay.'

The taxi arrived fifteen minutes later and they got in, Sam extracting directions from Bradley after only a few exasperatingly long minutes' interrogation, which he seemed to take as a further part of the test for being a real detective.

The taxi wound through the dark lanes, lulling Bradley towards sleep.

'Hey, Detective, don't nod off! I need instructions from you,' said Sam, but he gave up, deciding he'd wake Bradley when the lights of the town came into sight. He let his thoughts drift for a while, trying to think of other detective movie clichés he could use to confuse Bradley even further, before he realized they were driving uphill. Surely Fraxbridge was downhill, he thought, in the other direction . . .

As his suspicions began to grow he looked at the back of the taxi driver's head. They had not exchanged two words since they'd got in, Bradley eventually having stated their destination before slumping onto Sam's shoulder. Shaking off his own slight drunkenness, Sam saw that it was not the middle-aged man he would have expected, but in profile the driver was both female and definitely not young. He smelt the cigar smoke and saw the glowing tip as she puffed on her cheroot. He had just alarmingly concluded that they were being driven by a denizen of the granny mafia and was beginning to wonder where they might be going when they pulled into a car park near the top of the Hill.

Situated all round the edge of the car park, chillingly, were all the Austin Allegros, Citroën 2CVs and other granny cars that he had seen in the pub car park, except they were now many more in number. All their lights were ablaze, giving the surrounding night a deeper blackness and the tarmac surface the appearance of a floodlit sports pitch.

He urgently shook Bradley awake, who came to consciousness, slurring, 'Stick it on account, would you, taxpayer can pick this up . . .' and frowned bad-temperedly at Sam's efforts to keep him quiet.

'What's going on?' he asked.

'Your destination, gentlemen,' said their elderly driver, releasing the doors, which Sam hadn't realized had been auto-locked. He got out and pulled Bradley after him.

'No charge,' said their driver, puffing on her cigar and pulling away just fast enough so that the door shut itself, before reversing into the only space on the other side of the car park and completing a wall of motors facing them down.

'There's my car,' said Bradley, starting forward. 'Nice one!' But Sam grabbed his hand and held him back.

'Wait,' he said. 'Haven't you seen them?' He pointed at the bright lights, and slowly Bradley noticed the sound of revving motors. They were clearly standing at what had been designated a natural beauty spot, in a car park laid out so that tourists could look down over the valley from this high point. Bradley's car had been left by the fence right at the edge, above a sharp drop. He tried to shake off Sam's grip, but Sam held him even tighter, and now one of the cars came forward, turned until it was directly behind Bradley's vehicle and revved its engine harder than ever.

It burst forward with startling speed, raced up to the detective's Prius and smashed into the back of it, pushing it forward a yard or so, up against the fence.

'What the FUCK?! What are you doing, you old bitches?'

A second car now rammed the back of the Prius, making it press against the bulging fence until its bumper was over the precipice. Bradley had some thoughts of reaching it and driving it to safety, but before he could get to within twenty feet, a third struck it and then a fourth. The fence partially splintered and snapped, and as it came forward the nose of the car dipped down and slid underneath the twanging wires still dangling on the edge.

'Bitches!' yelled Bradley. 'My golf clubs were in there. I'll kick your hairy old arses!'

'Do you think maybe we should run away?' asked Sam, as a fifth car smashed into the back of the Prius. Its rear was now crumpled beyond recognition, and only remained visible for another second or so before the car wobbled violently and then slipped out of sight.

Bradley ran towards the fence, with Sam close behind. They couldn't see anything beneath the beams of the harsh lights behind them, but heard a heavy regular bouncing, crunching noise from the field below, mixed in with smashing glass as the car flipped over and over.

'They think they're going to get away with this?' asked Bradley, turning back to face the granny-motors. Several thoughts then occurred to both of them at once.

First, perhaps these old ladies weren't intending to leave any witnesses.

Second, if Sam and Bradley were found crushed near the remains of the car with a lot of alcohol in their blood-streams, perhaps no more explanation would be sought than the obvious one.

And third, even if foul play was suspected, no one would think to ask the harmless-seeming little old ladies of the village to show their garaged cars and prove their innocence.

These thoughts came in a lightning flash to both, encouraged by the sight that met them as they turned round: their former taxi driver was coming straight towards them, cigar clenched between her teeth that were showing through a wide grin, and at the end of her arm that was hanging out of the car window, a baseball bat going round in a sequence of threatening practice swings.

'This is it,' said Bradley. 'No more bullshit from the gimmers. It's action time!'

It was a nice sentiment, and Sam had about a second and a half to notice that it fitted perfectly with the grimly determined persona he had been trying to encourage Bradley to take on. However, it didn't make any difference to the fact that the old woman in question was doing forty miles an hour only a few dozen yards away when she pulled the handbrake, spun the wheel and, leaning out of the window, smacked the baseball bat across Sam's back with a two-handed swing that hit him so hard it picked him bodily up and neatly posted him over the fence into the darkness below.

'Sam!' shrieked Bradley, rushing to the edge. He could see nothing down there, and had no idea how far the drop was. What would he do without this new partner to tell him how to act? Just when he was starting to get into the role of a detective. He thought he heard a shout of some sort, but couldn't be sure.

Behind him the taxi driver laughed throatily as she gunned the motor and then drove away, leaving the space clear for whoever was next in line. Bradley saw another driver coming towards him, this time a meat cleaver in hand, and realized he had no choice. The engine behind him roared faster as it neared, and so without time to think he shut his eyes and leapt into the dark.

Heavy, life-long seconds seemed to pass in slow motion as he hung in the air and the freezing wind whistled past him. Then the ground smashed up into him, he tumbled, and when he came to a halt, he found himself to be on wet grass.

'Sam?' he shouted, looking around, waiting for the noise and the brightness to subside and let him get his bearings.

'Oh, that's nice,' came a voice from nearby. 'You decided to join me. I thought I was going to be stuck down here on my own. You haven't seen my left eyeball anywhere, by any chance?'

'Thank God, you're okay,' said the detective.

'I'm alive, but certainly *not* okay,' protested Sam. 'I've definitely broken at least five things. I don't know what exactly, but there are at least five of them.'

'What the fuck is going on?' wondered Bradley aloud as he looked back up to the car park, where the headlights were still shining out into the night above them. He put a hand to his head and stumbled in the direction of the voice. 'My wife's going to kill me,' he said.

'That would make a refreshing change, I must say. You know what, those drugs have finally worn off.'

'Don't worry,' said Bradley, 'I'm sure we can pick up some aspirin in town.'

'I wasn't talking about aspirin. I've *got* some aspirin on me, somewhere. Why is my first reaction at moments like this that I'd like to go to the pub?'

'Because you're an alcoholic.'

'Is that your foot, or am I being assaulted by a cow?'

'No, it's me. Here, get up. If we go downhill we should find the wreck of the car and then we can get my golf clubs to use in self-defence, if need be.'

It didn't take them long to locate the crumpled metal frame, which made quite a visible dark shape in the middle of the field, once their eyes had adjusted. The boot had popped open but had already been crushed in such a way that the clubs were trapped inside, mangled into strange and nasty-looking shapes.

'Driver,' said Bradley, handing it over.

'I don't want a driver, you have the driver. I'll go for a sand wedge – I reckon you could do some proper gouging with that.' Sam took the proffered club and lit the roll-up he had been making before sniffing suspiciously.

'Whatever you like,' said Bradley. 'What's that smell?'

'I was just wondering. Is it some sort of weed killer or crop spray or something?'

'It's *petrol*. Put that out!'

'Oh shit—' Sam threw the cigarette away from himself and both began to run as fast as they could, which was very slowly indeed, as running hurt them a great deal, and they hobbled and tripped on the little hummocks of the field. There was first a yellow light behind them, then a big whoosh and they felt the heat on their backs. They tried to put a few last yards behind them, then it came – a rippling boom that knocked Sam off his feet. Bradley turned round to face the blast of heat and saw the incongruously beautiful black-yellow-orange flames soaring up, and turning in on themselves, forming for one brief second a miniature mushroom cloud, then dissipating in the night air.

'That should satisfy them that the job's done, at least,' said Bradley, but the wry wisdom of the remark was somewhat undercut by the sunroof landing flat on his head and knocking him over.

'You're right,' said Sam. 'Look, the lights are going.'

A line of little old-lady shadows had been standing along the edge of the precipice looking down, silhouetted by the car lights, but one by one they started to melt away, and the lights to turn and drift down the side of the valley.

'How are we going to find our way back?'

'Piece of cake,' said Sam. 'Don't you have iPhones out here in the country?' He pulled the phone from his pocket, relieved to see it had survived the fall unscathed. Then they looked at each other, and Sam guiltily handed it over.

'Sorry,' he said, 'I don't know why I didn't think of that before. She must have knocked the sense out of me.'

Bradley dialled, hung up and dialled again, but could not get through. He handed it back.

'It's no good,' he said. 'We'll have to walk further until we get some coverage.'

'Map's not working either,' admitted Sam. 'But I don't think the town can be more than a mile down the hill. We just have to get to the other side of these woods and we should be able to see some sort of lights.'

They began to walk downhill, Bradley keeping ahead on the lookout for the treeline which they should soon enter, and they held their golf clubs up and ready in as menacing a pose as they could.

They soon came across what looked like some farm buildings and attracted the barking attention of a dog, making them skirt the property as widely as possible, going back uphill for a few hundred yards before turning south again. Soon they were at a fence and climbing into the woods.

'So, do you think that the old ladies killed Terry Fairbreath, then?' asked Sam.

'I'm not sure. I'd say whatever he was interested in, they are trying to keep secret. But whether that means they killed him, I don't know.'

'They've certainly got the intent to carry it out.'

'Well, yes, that is true. But maybe they scared him and he simply ran away.'

They had now been creeping silently through the woods for some minutes, and were thoroughly disorientated by the absolute darkness all around them. A large bruise was forming on top of Bradley's head, along with a decided headache compounded by the knock he'd received, the hangover that was setting in and thoughts of how he would explain all this to both his wife and his Superintendent. For his part, Sam didn't think he had broken any ribs, but he was pretty sure he had perforated a kidney, if that was the sort of thing that you could do by falling thirty feet or so into a field. Almost all of his back muscles were bruised. His calves ached, one knee had a nasty shooting pain in it and he still had absolutely no idea where he might go to sleep later on. If, that was, they survived the night.

Suddenly the trees seemed to clear and a small fraction of light peeped through from the night sky. A dark shape loomed above them, one that seemed large and out-of-place enough to make them both stop.

'What *is* that?' asked Sam. 'It's too tall to be a shed . . .'

'Or a hut,' said Bradley, blinking to get a better view. 'It's too dense to be a tree. It's sort of *man*-shaped.'

Bradley swung his golf club and thwacked it in the middle. 'It's soft,' he reported. 'Sort of like a huge rock made out of flesh.'

The object they were standing in front of then cleared the matter up by suddenly doubling in height, turning around on two giant legs, opening a mouth about as wide as a sofa and roaring.

'It's a bloody PERSON!' shouted Bradley, sprinting past it. Sam remained rooted to the spot, staring up at the furious face some thirty feet above and feeling that he was suddenly in the middle of one of Roald Dahl's nightmares.

'Run!' he shouted. Then he noticed that Bradley was nowhere to be seen, and that the creature had raised a fist angrily over its head. 'Shit!' he said, darting between its legs, and bolted down the hill.

That both had suddenly disappeared, slightly bewildered the creature for a moment, and they sprinted downhill to make as much headway as possible, hearing heavy footsteps and further roaring behind them. Feeling the need for silence was now at an end, and that being chased by an ogre was no time to maintain decorum, both screamed wildly as they sprinted and flung themselves over a solid wooden fence that appeared in front of them. They landed and rolled, and skidded down a bank, then staggered to their feet and looked upwards.

There was a beat of silence, then the ogre burst through the fence as though it was made out of nothing sturdier than a collection of breadsticks. They yelped again and ran on at full speed.

Finding themselves in the front yard of someone's country house, they flew in through the side door of an enormous, barn-sized garage. Locking it behind them, they then tiptoed to the back, crouched at the far end of the room and waited, hoping by some chance that the ogre might have been tricked or confused by their disappearance.

'What *is* that?' whispered Bradley.

'An ogre, I think.'

'An *ogre*?'

'Well, I think so. Or a really, really expensive children's toy gone wrong.'

Another extremely loud roar told them that their hiding place was not safe, and they saw the enormous creature tear through the garage's aluminium door as though it was no stronger than kitchen foil.

The two men mewed in fear, fell back and tumbled out of the back door that flew open as they fell against it. Finding the hillside still stretching out beneath them, they leapt and ran until they came to an ancient stone wall constructed of paving slabs. They clambered up, jumped down on the other side and found themselves standing on the verge of a road, then ran across and looked back tensely. This time, they felt, they might have been quick enough to evade the monster's notice.

It was with a mixture of abject fear and grinding inevitability that they saw the giant figure smash through the stone wall as though it had been made from nothing stronger than – well, you get the picture. It was flippin' strong.

They clutched each other. Between them here or there they might have let out a little squeak of terror, or an imprecation for their mummy to be near, or a regret at some life ambition that remained unfulfilled. But largely, as the gargantuan creature took one mighty step towards the road, they watched it in terrified and quaking silence.

Then, with a giant *whumf*, it disappeared.

Bradley and Sam continued holding each other and whimpering for a few more moments, inclined to believe that in the extremity of their terror it was their eyes or brains failing them, rather than the huge animal in human form (which might or might not be classified as an ogre) that had vanished.

Chapter Fourteen

GRADUALLY, as a minute or so passed and the animal failed to reappear, their breathing slowed, and Detective Inspector Bradley and Sam unlocked from each other's arms.

Cautiously they stepped forward until they were looking at where they had last seen the ogre standing.

'Odd,' said Bradley.

This was possibly something of an understatement, and Sam, who was a fan of understatement, but rarely managed it himself, cast the detective an admiring glance. They had crossed this short stretch of earth themselves only ten seconds before the ogre, and yet where firm earth had supported their footsteps, now there was quite clearly nothing but a large hole in the ground. It went down so far that there was no bottom, that they could see.

'*Very* odd,' agreed Sam. They listened out for the ogre for a minute or so, persuading themselves that they heard distant noises, but could not be sure. Then suddenly there came a deep rumbling below the ground that shook them off their feet again, and, crawling backwards at first, then getting up and running, they got as far away from the hole as possible.

'That noise was no ogre,' said the detective.

'It felt like an *earthquake*. What the hell is going on? There are no earthquakes in this part of the countryside.'

'Hey,' said Bradley. 'Let's stop this guy. Quickly!'

There was a station wagon coming along the road and they both frantically waved it down. The driver was a grey-haired middle-aged man, and he wound down his window.

'Thank God you stopped,' Bradley told the man. 'We desperately need a lift to Fraxbridge.'

'That's fine, I'm going that way,' said the man. 'Hop in.'

They got in and slumped back on the seats, hardly able to believe their luck.

'Thank God you came,' repeated Sam. 'We just narrowly avoided an assassination attempt by a gang of old grannies!'

'Oh, yes?' said the man, pulling off.

'Yes, but we got away.'

'Then my car exploded,' added Bradley.

'Oh dear,' said the man.

'And we got chased by a huge ogre.'

'An ogre, you say?' said the man, concentrating on his driving.

'Yes,' said Sam. 'Thirty feet tall, and able to smash a wall with its fists.'

'It was terrifying,' added Bradley.

'Doesn't sound very pleasant at all,' agreed the man.

'It wasn't! But luckily, just before it was going to get us and tear us into shreds, a huge hole appeared in the side of the hill and sucked it down.'

'Oh,' said the man.

'A huge hole,' added Bradley. 'Just like that, out of nowhere!'

'That's lucky,' said the man. 'Where you going to in Fraxbridge, then?'

'The police station,' said the detective glumly. He and Sam leant against the windows and stared out, watching what they could see of the countryside sliding by in the darkness.

'You mind if I put on Radio 3?' asked the man.

They both sighed.

Chapter Fifteen

A LOT OF THE TIME being insomniac could be a terrible affliction, thought Mrs Elizabeth Bottlescum, as the clock struck two and she climbed weary and sleepless from her bed to make her way downstairs. But even if one was just a humble old lady in a quiet little English village like this, there were small consolations. For instance, she thought as she climbed back up the stairs, she could perch here by the bedroom window with her bottle of sherry and her Sudoku puzzle on her knee, and watch the moonlit streets.

In these quiet hours there were many things she could contemplate and allow to wander through her mind. Her childhood in the north London suburbs; the family holidays in rugged, mountainous Scotland; those heartbreaking months of being sent away to live with strangers during the Blitz; and her husband's absolutely massive, colossal wanger. Thick as a milk bottle and as long as his foot. Amazing to behold. It was a wonder he could get about, she had often thought.

God, she missed that thing.

'HMS *Dreadnought*', he used to call it. That was a bit of a turn-off, of course. And the way he used to show off, using it to change channels on the television, or break empty the bottles of stout on the kitchen counter when he was one over the eight. Five bottles was his record. Bloody idiot.

'Come on, Pocket,' she said, pouring a splash of sherry into the cat's bowl.

She looked out over the rooftops, heard a distant rumble and saw the trees sway in a sudden gust of wind.

'That farting noise again,' she said. 'God knows where it's coming from. Horrible smell too.' Even in a quiet place like this, she thought, where people were supposed to have everything and be happy, there was always some trouble. She had seen what she was sure was a police detective pottering around – oops! Careful, she told herself. One mustn't use the word 'potter', all the residents knew that. She glanced at the large house at the top of the hill. One didn't want to displease the world-famous celebrity author who definitely *did not* secretly live in the locale. She nodded and raised her sherry glass.

'God bless you, ma'am,' she said, and drank a toast to the fortune that had flooded into the town since she had moved nearby. Admittedly it had meant those shops taking on ridiculous new names – Ye Olde Bakery and such like. She had kept an eye on the semi-secret gay porn parlour that Ralph Tingsdale was running out of his garage in the hope that he would put up a sign reading The Olde Bi-Curiositye Shoppe but to no avail.

It certainly was blissful living in such a beautiful small place as this. Quiet. Tranquil. And no immigrants. What's more, beneath the surface everyone was doing each other and trying to make money on the sly, while pretending to be terribly nice all the time. And if there was anything that Elizabeth Bottlescum loved (since the HMS *Dreadnought* had gone to the great ship-breaking yard in the sky) it was a seething hotbed of gossip.

And now there was a detective snooping around, asking questions! She scarcely dared wonder what he was likely to dig up. Who was it he was investigating? Oh yes, that Terry Fairbreath fellow. The thought half-stirred something in Elizabeth's memory and she frowned for a moment, but it refused to come. What was it now? Had *she* by any chance seen something? She was sure there was something there. Something about someone being on fire . . . Being shot at . . . Bows and arrows, perhaps . . . But quickly the images blurred with the John Wayne Western she'd been watching on the television the day before – which had been just super – and whatever she had been trying to think of was gone.

'If it comes, it comes,' she told herself. 'I can't force it.' She was getting terribly forgetful these days, it was true. There was that rhubarb pie she had left in the oven all night last week. And that boy she had found trapped down a well

– once she got home she popped the kettle on and then the thought went right out of her head and only came back a week later. Silly old ditz!

There came a sudden booming noise, startling her awake. Over the rooftops shone a bright jet of orange flame. She thought at first one of the houses had exploded, but then saw that the flame had taken the shape of an enormous dong-and-balls, flaming there in the sky.

'Oh, those wizard boys down at the school,' she chuckled to herself. 'Will the teachers never get them under control?' She leaned back in her chair, sherry in one hand and the other stroking Pocket on her lap. As her gaze rested on the huge cock in the sky, her mind naturally turned once more to the HMS *Dreadnought* and the adventures they used to have in the old days.

Gradually she fell into a doze, a smile on her lips and all thoughts of the fate of Terry Fairbreath quite forgotten.

Chapter Sixteen

When they reached Fraxbridge police station Bradley and Sam signed in and then went upstairs to sit and plan their next move. Bradley knew he should report all that had happened to his superiors and allow the law to take its course, but (on consultation with Sam as to the correct genre behaviour), he decided the case would likely be taken away from him, and he was determined to solve it on his own.

'I don't care if I have to kick arses and get in trouble,' he said, 'but I'll solve this goddamn case myself and damn the lot of them. How was that?'

'Pretty good,' said Sam.

'Okay, but I'd better fill this paperwork out first or I'll be for it,' he added, settling down to his desk and whistling away quietly to himself.

'You sure I can't help with anything?'

'No, it's just sixteen pages. I'll be fine, thanks.'

'Okay,' Sam sighed, 'I'll make a cup of tea, then.'

'Could I be terribly naughty and have a cup of ginseng?' asked Bradley.

'Lifestyle, *lifestyle*! You can have black coffee or nothing at all,' said Sam, walking off.

He sidled into the kitchen to find a kettle, and then sat in a free chair and watched Detective Brautigan. Although it was the middle of the night the station seemed to be packed. It appeared some big case was coming to a conclusion.

The superintendent was standing over Brautigan's desk, his sleeves rolled up, sweat patches under the arms, and with a weary expression. The desk itself was perhaps even worse than it had been yesterday. It was covered with piles of coffee- and ketchup-stained paperwork, photographs of mutilated corpses and cockroach-infested food cartons. In one corner was a mound of unexamined evidence piled in a heap, on top of which was a handgun in a lazily sealed evidence bag and a box with mysterious ticking coming from inside it. There also appeared to be a comatose prostitute handcuffed to one of the legs of the desk.

'So, you finally did it,' said the superintendent. 'You cracked the O'Shaughnessy case. He confessed! I never thought you could do it, you tough old bastard.'

Brautigan nodded wearily and rubbed his knuckles, still red-raw from the interrogation. 'The streets are going to be a safer place with that guy inside.'

'They sure will. Listen, Brautigan, you should take it easy now. You've only got one week until retirement. Take some time off. Reconnect with your wife, who you're separated from owing to your drink problem and depression. Maybe make a call to little Jenny, your four-year-old daughter, who you haven't seen in a long while.'

The superintendent sloped off, and Sam watched as Brautigan took a bottle of whisky from his bottom drawer, and went to top up his coffee with it, before changing his mind. Instead he found another cup, slurped whisky into it nearly to the brim, then diluted it with a splash of coffee in the top, turning it dark, and drank half in one gulp. He loosened his tie, rubbed a hand over his forehead and picked up the (recently replaced) phone.

'Is that Jenny? It's . . . it's Daddy,' said Brautigan, tears flowing freely over his enormous, rock-like face.

'That's right, Jenny, it's me, your old dad,' he said, his shoulders shaking with sobs that he managed to keep out of his voice.

'I wanted you to know that I love you, my little girl, and to say . . . Daddy's coming home. That's right! And I'm going to bring you a big doll to play with. The biggest doll in the whole wide world!'

'Have I really got to listen to this?' asked the prostitute, raising herself off the floor on one elbow.

'Just a minute, Jenny,' Brautigan said, pressing his hand

over the mouthpiece with elaborate care. 'SHUT THE HELL UP, YOU GODDAMN WORTHLESS PIECE OF CRAP, BEFORE I PUNCH YOUR STUPID HEAD OFF!' He unloosed his grip on the receiver and adopted the same saintly expression as before.

'That's right, Jenny, we'll have ice cream. Lots of ice cream. Chocolate, your favourite flavour! Okay, bye now. I love you . . .' He gently placed the receiver on its cradle without making a sound and sat back in his chair, taking a long deep breath and letting it out in a great sigh of relief.

Then another cop walked by his desk and dropped a file in front of him.

'Another prostitute murdered. The Full Moon Murderer strikes again. Guess O'Shaughnessy wasn't our guy after all . . .'

Brautigan's face crumpled.

Sam went over to check on Bradley and see if he was nearly finished.

'Yes, almost done,' said Bradley. 'Let's find somewhere to eat and talk over the case there. I can't concentrate with all this racket going on.'

They went out into the street just in time to see a typewriter smash out of an upper window and fall, along with a shower of glass, into the car park. It landed on a mattress that had been skilfully placed in exactly the right spot, and was scattered with other pieces of office furniture.

'There's an all-night cafe near the station,' said Bradley. 'At least I *hope* it's all-night — it would be unbearably depressing to have to sit in KFC at this time.'

'So,' SAID BRADLEY when they had sat down. 'I want to consult your experience of how these crimes work. You know more about this than me.'

'Okay. Right, what do you want to know?'

'What tips do you have about how an experienced detective would go about solving this, based on what we've seen?'

'It's not really a case in the classic mould, from what I've seen.'

'What do you mean?'

'Well, ideally, for a really juicy one, it would be a locked-room mystery.'

'I see — so the mystery is, who locked the door?'

'No, of course not. It's where a dead body is found behind a locked door, and the victim was clearly murdered. It's the purest kind of mystery.'

Bradley looked confused. 'I don't understand why. Surely the murderer just did the murder and then locked the door after him?'

Now it was Sam's turn to look confused. 'No, wait . . . Oh, right. The door's locked from the inside.'

'From the *inside*? But that's impossible!'

'Exactly, Detective. That's what makes it a profound mystery.'

'So what would the solution be?'

'From memory, it's a wild monkey that killed the victim and escaped up the chimney.'

Bradley pulled a police radio from his pocket and pressed the broadcast switch. 'DI Bradley to Sergeant Percival. Percival, you there?'

The receiver let out a short blast of static. 'Pschht! Receiving, Guv.'

'Er, it's me, Percival. Can you check round the nearby zoos, please, and see if there have been any monkeys that have escaped recently?'

'Psht. Yes, Inspector, no problem. Monkeys or all types of primate?'

'Er, just monkeys for now, thanks, Spencer. Unless they have gorillas small enough to fit down a chimney.'

'Pfffshhhhhhchtach! Down a chimney. Got that, Guv.'

'What are you doing?' asked Sam.

'Following your advice,' said Bradley. 'Why?'

'We haven't even found a body yet! I was just outlining the perfect murder mystery. Cancel that call.'

Bradley nodded and raised the radio again. 'Er, Bradley to Percival, are you receiving?'

'Pfffschhtt. Yes, Guv.'

'Cancel that last order. Stand down on the zoo search.'

'Psht. Got it, Guv. Call off the monkeys.'

'Over and out,' he barked into the radio. 'Sorry about that, Sam. It's just I've got to solve this case, you know? I haven't slept, I've been chased and beaten up, I'm hungover and eating terrible food. I feel like crap but it's exhilarating – I feel like a real cop, and God damn it I'm going to solve this case! How's your Zinger Tower Burger, by the way?'

'It's horrid. And I can't believe I got coleslaw as a side. I should have gone for beans – such a beginner's error. Now what I'm going to do is take you through the basic scenarios as I understand them, okay?'

Bradley nodded eagerly.

'Okay. So, there are a handful of conventional solutions to a dastardly murder such as which we may be ourselves investigating. If "such as which" is a phrase, and I'm too tired to work out whether it is or not.'

'Okay, great. Sock them to me,' said Bradley.

'Fine, so listen. Of all the solutions to murder mysteries, there are a number of famous solutions. Number one, the butler did it.'

Bradley was staring at him with such intensity he was practically goggling. He appeared to be making rapid mental calculations. Sam could readily understand that if he had spent his whole life as a village policeman, under the strict control of his wife (and he could hardly imagine what such a woman would be like), this must be the height of excitement. Bradley was wild-eyed, almost crazed-looking, like a teenager, thrilled and sleepless at their first festival.

For Sam's own part, he felt as fresh as a week-old cowpat. There were severe aches all the way up his back and legs. He had firmly come down from whatever that pill had been and had a hangover from the four pints and six whiskies he'd drunk earlier. Now he was dehydrated, tired, demoralized, scared, feeling queasy and short-tempered and meanwhile Bradley was making a spectacle of them both into the bargain. As far as he could tell, he was in need of just about every kind of medical and spiritual encouragement that the world had to offer, and his mental checklist of immediate needs ran something like this, in no particular order:

A crap.

A drink.

Three or four pints of water.

At least twelve hours of sleep in a comfortable bed.

Several thousand pounds.

As many strong painkillers as would likely not prove fatal.

A hot bath.

A massage.

A week in Spain.

A good novel.

Some *excellent* food.

He decided that a rest break was in order and, warning Bradley that he would be a few moments, retired to the disabled toilets of the KFC.

This might be the moment to reflect that none of us knows what others get up to in toilets once the doors are locked. We may suspect various unedifying and morally regrettable acts, but we never can know. And for some people (Sam being one of these) the very act of clicking the lock into place turned the drab, square, white-tiled space into a temporary home, where for a few minutes he might act exactly as he pleased without making concession to any idea of normality. Therefore, with the pain ringing all the way up and down his legs at every step like a pianist running the back of his hand up and down the keyboard, Sam first removed his mud-soaked socks and shoes, then splashed his poor feet with water from the sink and dried them with paper towels.

'If there's one thing I know how to do,' he muttered, 'it's take a rest break.'

He took a miniature of Jameson from an inside pocket, cracked it open and downed it in two swift glugs. Then he refilled it from the tap and swigged down three strong ibuprofen. It was the first peace and quiet he had known since arriving in the allegedly peaceful countryside, and silence beckoned him to rest his head on the cistern for a moment, when he lost consciousness. He roused himself what felt like a second later, with an unsettling doubt in the back of his mind that fifteen or forty-five minutes might easily have passed, and so he concluded his business as quickly as he could, tipping out a long thick line of the white powder he had been sold the previous day, wondering for a minute if there was not substantially less than he remembered when he'd bought it, then cast the doubt aside and hoovered it up in a quick, stinging snort.

Exiting the room a minute or so later (and briefly casting glances left and right to detect any suspicious looks coming from others), he asked for three large cups of tap water and one of orange juice from the counter. He sat alongside Bradley, who didn't seem even mildly perturbed by the wait (however long it had been), and was talking rapidly into his phone. The detective seemed excited rather than scared, so Sam concluded he either wasn't talking to his wife, or he was, and with his altered persona had already established some ground-breaking new protocols with her.

Sam's restoration was nearly complete, but still lacking its final ceremony, which he now enacted with as much solemnity and care as if he had been celebrating a sacrament. Setting the four cups in front of him, he cracked an extra-strong Alka-Seltzer into the first cup of water, and poured a sachet of Dioralyte into the second. The third he gulped straight down and then sipped the orange juice as he let the two potions settle. Then, once his arid system had absorbed the first cup's worth of water (which took about ninety seconds), he demolished the hangover cure and the diarrhoea treatment in short measure.

The powder was kicking in, too. There seemed a small chance that (back pain aside) in fifteen minutes' time he might start to feel all right. Bradley was still muttering away on his phone, and Sam felt no immediate need to interrupt him, so he glanced around, and after spotting a familiar face not two tables away, had to do a movie-style double-take.

'Good Lord! Literally. It's Lord Ickham.'

Without raising himself from his hunched position over a paper plate of rapidly disappearing spicy wings, Horace glanced up from a nearby table and looked urgently around the room with a hunted expression, apparently unsure of what he had heard. Then his eyes fell on Sam, and his unease vanished at once.

'Dear boy,' he said, smiling as he wiped his mouth with a napkin. 'You remembered the old moniker. No longer accurate, I'm afraid.'

'Oh dear. They haven't stripped you of it already?' Sam had a sudden worrying vision of a highly publicized drugs scandal on the benches of the House of Lords.

'Good *heavens*, no! They don't actually do that, do they? No, quite the reverse. Another promotion, as you would put it.'

'Blimey, well done!' Sam said. 'What are you up to now?'

'Earl of Cheltenham. Poor old Chummy Rawlinson, my cousin, was the last Earl. He passed away.'

'Your *cousin*,' said Sam, feeling this warranted more gravity than a great-uncle of 107. 'I *am* sorry.'

'Well, you needn't be. I never met the man – he moved to Brooklyn after that Profumo thing blew up. When I say "poor old Chummy", I mean just that – he was very poor and very old, so I can't see that we would have exactly got on like a house on fire. Which is, ironically, how he died – smoking in bed.'

'A dreadful habit. I smoke in the bath, because that doesn't seem quite as dangerous.'

'I quite agree. Hey, by the way, are you okay for, er . . .'

'Naughty salt?' said Sam, breaking out what he had once heard was the posh phrase for cocaine, and then immediately realizing he was a suck-up of the worst kind. 'You're very generous,' he said, 'but I just had some. Is this your usual sort of joint?'

'At two a.m. it is, when you've got the raging munchies.'

'But haven't you got . . . well, a staff of about two hundred and twelve in your house?'

'Quite possibly. But I'm not waking cook up in the middle of the night, Sam. It's so bloody uncouth.'

'And you can't knock something up yourself?'

'Naturally, I bloody can! They had me on that *Master Celebritychef* thingy last year. The Aussie declared my smoked ham and puréed pea ravioli to die for. But the big bald one and I didn't get on.'

The aristocrat, although he spoke with the fluency that his very expensive education had instilled in him, betrayed all the other signs of being insensibly stoned – once a pause of more than a second descended on their conversation, his attention wandered away so that Sam was able to watch, amused, as Horace's mind flitted from wonderment and absorption in the posters and menus printed on the wall, to skulking, paranoid glances at the other diners.

At last it seemed that Bradley was finished on the phone, because now he turned a face towards Sam that was beaming with pride.

'It's all sorted,' he said.

'What is?' asked Sam suspiciously. 'What have you done? I thought we were halfway through a conversation.'

Bradley shrugged this off. 'Percival arranged it for me. The butlers,' he explained. 'I've had them all brought in.'

Chapter Seventeen

LOTS OF QUESTIONS filled Sam's mind, but the first of them to find voice was: 'How the hell long was I in the loo for?'

'Quite a while, actually. A good hour. I did begin to wonder what was going on. Did you fall asleep or something?'

'That's not important,' said Sam. 'Why have you arrested all the – and, wait a minute, what do you mean by "all the butlers", anyway? Who actually *has* butlers?'

'Oh, quite a lot round here. Lord Selvington has at least two. The mayor lives in a huge house, owned by his wife, and he has one. Judge Barnstable . . .'

Sam was about to insist that he let them go at once, but Bradley's radio crackled with a question from Percival. 'That's right, Sergeant. Hose them down!'

'Let's get back there at once,' said Sam.

'Damn right,' said Bradley. 'I'm going to nail this mother!'

They ran out into the street in time to see Horace

reversing his open-top 1930s sports car clean onto the pavement and then screech off down the road in an S-shape before bursting onto the local green, skirting a pond and diving over a hill out of sight. Bradley and Sam ran as fast as they could to the police station.

When they got there, they sprinted straight through to the cells at the back of the building. There were around twenty butlers of all different ages, shapes and sizes, but right now they had one thing in common: rather than place them in individual holding cells, Sergeant Percival had instead lined them up along the back wall, forced them to strip to their underwear and was training the thick unflinching jet of a fire hose upon them.

With deep alarm, Sam was taking in the personage of Sergeant Percival for the first time. He was tall and lean, with dark brown eyes that showed a fixed satisfaction in his task, and a mouth set in a grim half-smile. Here, Sam could tell, was someone who truly loved being a policeman.

'Um, excuse me,' said Sam, tapping him on the shoulder. Percival looked askance at this interloper who would interrupt his enjoyment, and evaluated him coolly up and down, quite obviously wondering whether there was a pretext under which he could throw him in with the butlers. 'I think you're drowning that one,' said Sam, pointing to a fat old man in the corner, who was lying on his side, eyes bulging open, his mouth hanging wide as twenty gallons of water splashed into it each second. Percival did not respond for a moment or so, then reluctantly turned the hose to the others, some of whom looked like they were starting to get too dry. The noise in the room was a kind of constant roaring above which the screams and imprecations of the butlers could hardly be heard.

'Good work, Percival!' said Bradley, clapping him on the shoulder. 'Remarkable work. As efficient as ever.' Percival nodded thanks towards his superior without taking his eyes off the victims.

'Can I have a word with you?' asked Sam.

Bradley led him into a nearby open cell, where the noise was less deafening. He was still as wide-eyed and keyed-up as before, and clearly excited about undertaking his first interrogation. In fact, he was rubbing the knuckles of one of his hands in preparation.

'What the *fuck* have you done this for?' Sam begged him. 'I was only telling you a *list* of potential candidates. Didn't you realize?'

Bradley stared at him, showing no signs of comprehension. Sam thought back to a doubt that had first occurred to him in the KFC bathroom an hour before, and began to wonder about something.

'You haven't searched my pockets, have you?'

'I had to. You're not a policeman. You turned up on the

very day that Fairbreath was reported missing. I had to regard you as a suspect.'

'Okay,' admitted Sam. 'That is good police work. But you didn't . . . *take* anything that you found there, did you?'

Bradley's look changed to one of smug amusement. 'I'm doing it, you see?' he said. 'I'm really becoming the cop you told me to be. I'm drunk, and now I'm on drugs!'

'Oh my God!' said Sam, putting a hand to his face. 'The butlers *didn't* do it,' he said as slowly and loudly as he could, staring straight into Bradley's eyes. 'You have to release them at once. Then let's go upstairs and drink lots of water, have some coffee and I'll explain.'

Bradley seemed to understand there might be some bad implications for him in all this, but was still clearly buzzing as he went back out and switched off the emergency fire hose at the source. Percival turned round, enraged, and was visibly disappointed to see it was his boss who had turned it off.

'Send them home, Percival,' said Bradley. 'The butlers are to be released without charge.' Percival's face dropped, and he started ordering the soaked men to fetch their clothes back from the pile where they had been left in one of the cells.

'You're in *deep* trouble!' one of the men was shouting. 'I told you quite clearly, I'm not even a butler. My name is

Butler. *Jon* Butler! And I'm a big deal round here. You'll regret this, mark my words!'

'Get them in the van as quick as possible, Percival,' said Bradley. 'But don't use the hose again, just the stick will do. So, explain,' he said, turning back to Sam. 'I thought the butler did it.'

'*No!* Listen. That's only one of many scenarios. I was starting with the least likely – I didn't think there were any butlers any more. The next surprise solution for any crime novel is that the policeman did it.'

'Uh-huh,' said Bradley, nodding.

'You see? I'm just running you through the possibilities. Now, let me fetch that coffee and we'll sit down and talk this through further. I don't want to get you into more trouble.'

Sam wandered wearily upstairs and, eschewing the poisonous coffee machine in the corridor, found some dregs of instant in the bottom of a jar at the back of a cupboard. He boiled the kettle and made two cups of strong black coffee, tipped a small landslide of sugar into each, stirred and carried them back downstairs, thinking how cross he was that above everything else, Bradley had taken some of his mystery drugs.

At the bottom of the stairs, silence greeted him.

He stood in the middle of the carpet holding the two

Styrofoam cups and looking around. There was not a whisper. He didn't doubt Percival's ability to get the thirty soaked, humiliated and outraged men dressed and into the back of a van in under five minutes. But there had been several other cops milling about – the desk sergeant, the superintendent and Brautigan, to name only a few. He walked forward into the cells and heard nothing but the dripping of water from fittings that had been splashed.

No one.

Then he noticed that something *was* different. All the cell doors were closed. And here were the keys, in the nearest door. He walked to it and looked in. There was Bradley, busy handcuffing himself.

'What are you doing?' asked Sam.

'Just what you said.'

'That's *not* what I said, you drugged-up lunatic! That's specifically *not* what I bloody said.'

'Just turn the keys in the lock, if you will,' said Bradley in a tone of saint-like humility. 'I'll do my time. I understand how these things work – at least, I think I do. I did the murder myself and the others have been covering it up for me . . .'

A thought struck Sam as he wandered back out, and he went over to another cell door, popped open the peephole and saw what he had feared. Brautigan was in there, brooding with incredible intensity, like a bull about to pounce or an avalanche before it falls. Before Sam could move away, he leapt forward, reached his hand through the hole and clasped Sam's head in a pincer grip between forefinger and thumb, crushing his brain.

'You better let me out of here,' he growled, 'or I'll pull you in through this letterbox and turn you into dog food.'

'Understood, Mr Brautigan, sir,' said Sam. 'I'm working on it. Just give me another moment or two!'

The grip released him and he fell to the floor, from whence he got back to his feet, returned to Bradley's cell and made his feelings very clear: that Bradley was to release all his colleagues.

'I can't do that,' Bradley said. 'I'm a policeman, and it's my duty to detain myself and my colleagues if we're guilty.'

'But you're *not* bloody guilty!' Sam shouted. 'Well, you are, of many things, but not of murder. Or not of *this* murder. So go and unlock the other cells right this damn instant! I'll be outside until Brautigan has had time to calm down, and you've explained yourself to your other officers.'

Sam walked outside and sat on a wall, partly to enjoy his coffee in peace, partly to intercept anyone who tried to come into the police station in the next five minutes so he could detain them for a while as things were being sorted out, and finally, also to get some cool air to his head after its assault by Detective Brautigan.

The light was beginning to show in the eastern sky when Bradley found him again and invited him back inside.

'I understand,' he said. 'I've been overzealous. I've talked things over with the superintendent, and I've got search warrants for the properties of all the old grannies, and warrants for their arrest, all getting ready right now – I just need their names. I want you to finish telling me your plan as we drive over there, and I'll be making enquiries as to their identities.'

'Okay, no problem,' said Sam as they went through to the car park and got into a new car assigned to Bradley. He was starting to feel tiredness weigh on him. 'Look, shall we finish this stuff off?' he suggested. 'In for a penny, after all.'

'Right on, brother,' said Bradley, as he took the packet, squeezed it in the crook of his hand so it popped open, lowered a nostril to it and took a long deep lungful. A huge pile of white powder disappeared – Sam would have complained, but it was too late, and he didn't know if he was that concerned anyway. He winced, coughed, wiped his nose, popped on the stereo and, feeding a CD into it, pressed play. The relaxed funk of Curtis Mayfield filled the car, playing 'Pusherman'. Sam guzzled the rest as Bradley gunned the engine.

'How did Brautigan take it?'

'That guy?' said Bradley as the drugs set in. 'He was okay.'

'Really? He didn't try to kill you for locking him up?'

'*Him*? No way! He's crippled by guilt for all the years of bad things he's done.'

'He didn't seem that way to me,' said Sam, feeling his temples. 'He seemed pretty angry.'

'He just needed the law laid down to him. That punk just needs treating with a firm hand.'

'You're getting into this, aren't you?'

'Damn right I am,' said Bradley. 'Besides, Brautigan?' He shook his head. 'A ticking time bomb.'

'He certainly is that.'

'No, I mean that thing on the corner of his desk. It's literally a ticking time bomb – that's his lazy approach to dealing with evidence for you. He hasn't even looked at it yet – could go off at any second.'

As he said this there was an enormous booming explosion above them. All the windows on the first floor blew out, and flames licked the side of the building as debris fell all around them.

'You see?' said Bradley. 'I tried to warn him.'

The detective put the car into gear and pulled away quickly, avoiding bricks and falling masonry that crushed a hole in the tarmac behind them. He turned into the street at fifty miles an hour and tossed a police radio into Sam's lap.

'Shouldn't we do something?' the writer asked.

'That's a case for the fire department,' said Bradley. 'And nothing's getting in the way of me solving this case right now. Use that, call the ambulance and fire engine to get over here. That button on the bottom right gets you through to regional emergency services.'

Sam did so at once, then rang off as they were reaching the edge of town and asked, 'Is there a twenty-four-hour booze place round here?'

'In a town like this? No way! Look under your seat, motherfucker,' said Bradley.

Sam looked puzzled as he rummaged around and then adopted a look of awe as he pulled out a bottle of rum.

'Confiscated it from the evidence locker,' said Bradley.

Sam cracked it open, took a swig and offered one to the detective, who drank deeply and then gave the bottle back.

'An honour to work with you, Detective,' he said. They were now speeding through the dawn countryside; the hills, the fields, the waterways and woods lit up by the copper sunlight of very early morning. The effect was enhanced, of course, by the fact that they were now both buzzing so hard that their very vision shimmered before them.

'That stuff's good,' said Bradley.

'Yeah, man,' said Sam.

'Oh yeah,' said Bradley.

'So let me tell you how it works, then,' said Sam, feeling garrulous. 'I've given you two classic endings – the butler did it, the detective did it. The next one in line is, *everyone* did it.'

They were doing about eighty when they neared the turning for Mumford, and Bradley hardly slowed as he hit the corner and scorched up the hill towards town.

'That's a very good hypothesis,' said Bradley.

'It's *not* one. How many times do I have to say? Hey, who the hell's that coming up behind us?'

'The grannies, the Parish Council, the librarian . . . They've all got something to hide,' said Bradley, looking determined.

'You're not to take this as your new theory,' warned Sam. But the car behind had taken up all of their attention. It was approaching them fast – and they were doing almost ninety miles an hour. Now it began to weave from side to side, nudging ahead, then revving its engine and swerving to the other side to get through. Bradley made no evasive manoeuvres, but his necessary movement in the narrow, tree-shrouded, winding lane made it appear he was deliberately blocking its passage, and the other driver became more dangerous and erratic as his speed grew.

'What's he playing at?' said Bradley. 'He must be one of them, trying to stop us . . .'

'No . . .' warned Sam. They were nearly at the little town's main street now, and neither car had slowed down. Bradley picked up his radio.

'Percival? DI Bradley to Sergeant Percival?'

There wasn't even the beat of a pause. The reply came crackling through at once.

'Pshhhhft. Percival here.'

'We are now to regard the entire population of Mumford as suspects. This is a town at war. And we are at war with it.'

'Pshtshhht. Understood.'

'They have tried to cover up a murder. They tried to kill a police officer once, and are now trying again. Get everyone. I mean EVERYONE! I want this town surrounded!'

'Keep your bloody hands on the wheel!' shouted Sam.

But it was too late. The lane opened up, the overhanging trees vanished, and all of a sudden they were careening across the middle of the square, braking hard but still doing upwards of seventy. Then sixty, fifty . . . But the shops on the other side were approaching rapidly. They turned, skidded, both cars forming a pirouette and their tyres *ther-dududing* over the cobbles. Sam crouched and pulled his hands over his head, seeing the pink painted shopfront of Mrs Stainwetting's Teae Shoppe loom above him.

Then there was a crash. He pulled his hands ever more tightly over his head, expecting falling glass to cut through them, and thinking all sorts of thoughts at once: that he'd never play 'Moonlight Sonata' again; that being able to play 'Moonlight Sonata' had never really got him anywhere in the first place, and his energies might have been better invested elsewhere; that he had never been in a fulfilling relationship; that the previous fact probably had at least in part something to do with his lifestyle and he really ought to sort himself out if he came through this; that by sorting himself out he meant cutting down to nothing stronger than smoking weed and drinking port; that there must be a small chance he'd get a sexy scar out of this car crash; that he had never found a satisfactory answer to the impenetrable mystery of why Fritz Lang had made two film noirs back to back in the mid-1940s with such similar plots and with an almost identical cast (Edward G. Robinson, Joan Bennett, Dan Duryea); that there must be a chance he would get cut in half and still be awake to see his own guts spilling about the place.

Then he passed out.

Chapter Eighteen

IT MUST HAVE been some time before he woke again. As he
came round he expected to find himself peering up into
familiar but withered faces telling him that he had been in a
coma for sixty years, or to be feeling around for an amputated limb. But the fact that he was upside down and felt his
face pressed against a cold marble floor signalled to him that
he had not been urgently whisked to hospital, or tended to
and mended by educated and loving hands.

He rolled on his side, then got up. The detective's car
was sticking in through the plate-glass window of the tea
shop. Sam had been thrown clear, attracting to the surface
of his clothes a certain amount of broken glass and whipped
cream, and to the rest of his body a number of new and
unexpected aches. He rested against the counter and ate a
chocolate eclair, first taking certain shards out of it. Then he
lit a cigarette, climbed over the wreckage and walked into
the square.

The sight that greeted him was, to his mind, out of a

Paul W. S. Anderson movie. Which may not be a universal analogy, so the author will elucidate.

Helicopters were flying above, armed troops marching in formation over the south side of the square, and the denizens of Mumford were to a man, woman and child lined up in front of the Town Hall with their arms behind their heads. Searchlights flitted across the paving stones from hovering gunships.

Ahead of him was a figure he recognized and so he stumbled forward, only to be suddenly surrounded by SWAT officers, assault rifles at their shoulders, their voices screaming for him to get on the ground. He did so, and welcomed the relief from his aching legs and back, and the cold of the stone beneath his cheek.

'Wait, wait!' shouted a voice, running closer. 'That's my partner. Let him go! Help him up!'

Rough, gloved hands grabbed Sam beneath the armpits and hoisted him reluctantly to his feet. He found himself face to face with Bradley.

'You okay?' asked the detective.

'It's you,' Sam said weakly. 'I thought I was in the film *Minority Report* or something. Or that short story by Ray Bradbury, what's it called . . .'

'Snap out of it, man!' shouted Bradley, giving him a slap. 'We've got our miscreants. It was the whole town, as you said. *Everyone*'s the murderer.'

'Wait a minute,' said Sam, struggling to make himself heard above the beating of the rotor blades in the air above, the loudhailers shouting orders to troops all around and the heavy grinding of the tank tracks as they moved through the streets, crushing the cobbles beneath their weight.

'I didn't *say* everyone did it,' said Sam. He could see Bradley was struggling to hear him and so he beckoned him over to a nearby shop that was open – a pharmacy that had been given the improbable title of Ye Olde Cure-iosity Shoppe (Chemist). They stepped through the broken windows and made their way to the back of the shop.

'I've got bad news for you,' said Sam, sitting down.

Bradley didn't seem able to concentrate. He kept answering queries from the radio on his belt and giving further invasive orders for the town to be searched and cut off. Looking around himself in dismay, Sam suddenly saw this as a great opportunity, the kind he had never had before. Bradley was still distracted as Sam searched along the shelves. He took effervescent vitamin supplements, aspirin, paracetamol, ibuprofen, hangover cures, extract of milk thistle, chewing gum, Lockets, children's cough syrup (for nostalgia's sake) and anything else he could find, until his pockets were full. Then he saw a kettle in the back room, boiled it and made himself a cup of extra-strength flu remedy, which not only tasted nice but was always good for getting a bit high.

'So,' said Bradley, finally switching off his radio set. 'Oh, thanks,' he said, accepting a cup of Lemsip. 'What's the news?'

'I hadn't *finished*,' said Sam. 'I *told* you I hadn't finished running through the various options for who's done it!'

'But we've got all the old ladies. Five cars found with bashes on them, and when we've interviewed everyone we'll be able to tie them all together.'

'Fine,' said Sam. 'But we haven't solved Terry's disappearance, have we? I haven't told you the next in the sequence of people who might have done it.'

'You mean there's more?'

'Of course there is! Come on, follow me . . .' With the windows blown out, the chemist's shop was not much quieter than the street. Holding his mug, Sam walked forward through the rubble of the front window and studied the suspects all lined up. They looked as if they were ready to be shot, which sent a chill down his spine. He spotted a nearby police car and walked towards it, hoping there at least it would be quiet enough to talk without feeling one's head was about to explode. Bradley was dawdling, talking on his radio again, and Sam took this opportunity to dart over to the car wreck he had crawled out from and search around in it until he found the rum bottle. Unbroken.

'A victory,' he whispered. 'Another victory for me against the universe. Fuck you, world!' He realized that he must still be a little bit high as he raised the bottle to the sky and attracted not only the attention of everyone from the town, but also the thirty or so armed officers who happened to be milling about, and half a dozen concealed snipers, the red aiming spots of whose rifles suddenly appeared on his chest.

He waved his arms over his head in surrender.

'Okay,' he said slowly. 'Sorry, nothing to worry about, I'm DI Bradley's partner.' The red spots vanished and the SWAT team wandered off, looking for other targets, and Sam returned to the car, plucking his cup of Lemsip from the roof and getting in the back, wondering if there were any health implications about mixing these things together.

'Hello, old bean,' said a familiar voice.

Sam already had the rum bottle almost to his lips and turned his head somewhat comically towards the man next to him, in the awareness of having been caught out. He heard a laugh.

'You go ahead. I'm not in a position to suggest that's inappropriate, even if I wanted to. Look . . .' It was Horace, holding up his hands, which were handcuffed together.

Sam took a good long swig of the rum, then handed it over to the prisoner and sipped his hot drink.

'It was me driving that car behind you. Terribly glad you weren't badly hurt,' said Horace.

'But we saw you driving off ages before that.'

'In the wrong direction. I was stoned out of my mind. I woke up in a little lane ages later and decided to race it back.'

'Jesus,' said Sam. 'We're not very grown up, are we?'

'No,' said Horace, looking down. 'I'm not.'

'I wasn't being posh by using the first person plural, Horace,' said Sam. 'I meant both of us. *We're* not very grown up.'

'It's true,' admitted the aristocrat.

'You have to act up to the role, and get used to being the Earl of Cheltenham.'

'Ah,' said Horace.

'Ah?'

'Not strictly accurate, once again. I got a call half an hour ago.'

'Another promotion?'

He nodded sadly. 'Dear second-cousin-thrice-removed Philomina.' With handcuffed hands he awkwardly doffed the homburg that he was wearing at rather a jaunty angle (the only angle to wear it, Sam expected he would say), and clutched it to his heart, gazing heavenwards with a noble air.

'Old?' Sam asked.

He nodded happily.

'Distant?'

Once again Horace gaily signalled that this was indeed

the case. 'Couldn't be more distant. New Zealand, South Island. Shacked up with a lumberjack over there, the randy old biddy.'

'I feel a quote is in order about how the Lord takes us when he feels it is right.'

'Yes,' he reflected, 'but then, that's probably balls. She was killed by a falling tree that showed certain signs of having been tampered with by a chainsaw. Naughty hubby was after her inheritance.'

'So what does that make you?'

'Duke of Rochester. Fancy a line?'

'No, come on . . .' said Sam, wondering whether he could have smuggled drugs past his arresting officer, and then reflecting he almost certainly could. But taking drugs while *in* a police car seemed to him to be perhaps beyond innocent fun, and possibly straying into the area of actually asking for trouble. A little pouch of white powder was offered to him.

'This is ridiculous,' he thought, licking his finger and dabbing it so that it was frosted all over with crystals. 'But we'll all be dead one day,' was ever the answering thought, and so he sucked the acrid powder from his finger and chased its sickening taste down his throat with a large gulp of rum.

'By the way, do you remember asking me about an ogre?' said Sam.

Horace suddenly looked suspicious. 'This wasn't some dreadful children's book you were pitching to me, was it, in the hope that I'd send it on to my publisher?'

'No, it bloody wasn't! A *real* ogre. Or as real as a – well, whatever. You asked me if I'd seen one. We ran into him.'

'Oh!' said the aristocrat, jerking up in his seat.

'Literally,' added Sam, wishing, parenthetically, that the occasional and accurate use of this word still had the power it deserved, and adding, just to make his point, 'I practically stuck my hand up his bum. And Detective Einstein over there tried to brain him with a mashie. Or a niblick, or whatever it was. This white stuff does make you talkative, doesn't it?'

'It has that effect.'

'But my question was, if you knew about this bloody great mystical creature roaming the woods, why didn't you warn us?'

'Well, I didn't know for sure, did I? I saw it myself a couple of months back when I was out foraging for mushrooms.'

'That doesn't sound like you.'

'*Magic* mushrooms. I'd hidden my stash somewhere in the woods to prevent Mother from getting her hands on it again – she posts some dreadful shit on Twitter when she's high. Supporting House of Lords reforms, that sort of thing. But I was high as a goose when I buried it, and I couldn't find the stuff sober, so got tooty again and went out looking for it in that state. I thought he was a hallucination, but then as I drove away, he took a bite out of the old jalopy the size of a dinner plate that was still there in the morning. So I got sort of confused. Now I come to mention it, he did seem a touch on the dangerous side. How did *you* escape?'

'Well, when he was in the middle of trying to turn us both into human tartare, a hole opened up on the side of the hill and swallowed him whole.'

'I sometimes wonder if it would be easier to get to the bottom of all this if one was a bit more sober some of the time,' confessed Horace.

'That is possibly true,' agreed Sam, peering out of the window at the town square, which was to his eyes bright-lit with neon lights and zigzagged in zany ways upon his retinas. 'So you've no idea where the damned thing came from?'

'The school, I expect,' said Horace. 'I don't know how these thickos fail to notice it, but it's obviously a school that teaches witchcraft of some sort. Anyway, I'm very sorry for your trouble, and glad you're safe. But . . . A *hole*, you say – and it opened up just like that. *Another* one!'

'There have been others?'

'A few years ago a semi-detached house vanished into a hole that suddenly appeared at the top of the town, near the base of the hill. It was never really investigated, they had it all hushed up. Terry Fairbreath was terribly interested in all this, I seem to recall.'

'Interesting,' said Sam. 'Here, Bradley's coming over.'

'Better hide the old snort.'

'No, give him some. He could do with it. But don't mention you knew the ogre was out there – that might be a bit of a sore spot.'

Bradley got into the car.

'Want some drugs?' asked Horace.

'Who the fuck are you?' the policeman asked, whipping the proffered packet out of his hand and examining the contents.

'Uh, nobody. Well, we met before. And then I nearly killed you earlier, and you arrested me. That's why I'm in your car, at least.'

'Oh, yeah. *You*,' said Bradley, dunking his nose into the crystals. 'Can you keep your posh mouth shut for ten seconds while I talk to Tinker Bell over there on the other seat?'

'Not a problem,' Horace said cheerily, for which he received a slap.

'I said *shut*,' said Bradley. Horace nodded dumbly.

Sam leant forward and offered the bottle of alcohol. The detective partook largely of it and then once more of Horace's powder, the latter so much so that on receiving his packet back, Horace stared at its emptiness with outrage for a moment and articulated several violent oaths without using his vocal cords. Sam felt a pride at Bradley's new attitude swell in his heart.

'So tell me,' said the detective.

'There are *other* solutions,' Sam said. 'Not just that everyone did it.'

'Such as what?'

'Well, now,' said Sam. 'I would say "please don't overreact" but I suppose we're past the point where that would be a helpful request. If it's not the butler, and not the detective, and it wasn't everyone acting in collusion, then . . .' Sam reflected an instant too late that this new Bradley, this monster who was a creation of his, would not respond to what he was about to say. He had to finish the sentence.

'In my experience of crime novels, which you are asking about,' said Sam, 'it could be the narrator.'

Bradley didn't even say a word. He opened his car door, got out, walked round, opened Sam's door, yanked him out (spilling his drink) and slammed his head four times against the bonnet.

'Don't fuck me around!' he shouted. 'You're holding out on me!'

'I'm not!' yipped Sam, his face squished against the police car. 'It's a clever ending if the innocent-seeming narrator turns out to have done the murder.'

Bradley yanked on his arm and spun the young man

round. He looked at him, and saw that Sam was being honest and was trying to be helpful. He grabbed a handful of his T-shirt and lifted him off his feet.

'What the FUCK does "it could be the narrator" mean?'

'It depends if we are characters in a novel that is written in the first or third person. Guessing that it's third person, then the narrator is of course the murderer in every whodunnit ever written. And even if they were a first-person narrator, we wouldn't be able to tell who it is.'

'Meaning what, in relation to my inquiry?' asked the detective.

'Okay,' admitted Sam. 'Meaning that that remark wasn't any use to you at all. It's meaningless.'

Bradley let him go so he smacked into the cobblestones, and rubbed his arse as he got up.

'I was only trying to give you a list of potentials,' said Sam pathetically, as the world spun counter-clockwise.

Bradley pointed to the car door. Sam got in and Bradley walked back round to his front seat.

'So what else is there?'

'Okay. As you can imagine, we've exhausted the conventional solutions. If you really want to know, the next idea would be that we aren't in a murder inquiry at all.'

'Meaning?'

'Occam's razor. Follow the evidence to the least unlikely solution: we've got no body, so there was no murder.

Terry's out there somewhere, still alive. Maybe he's run off because of tax problems, or had a fall and got amnesia. Maybe he killed himself.'

'No way!' said Bradley. 'I'm following my intuition, just as you told me to. I can feel in my gut there's been a murder here and I'm going to find my way to the heart of this.'

'Okay,' said Sam, somewhat hopelessly. 'What else can I say?'

'Give me the next solution you can come up with.'

'These solutions are from *fiction*, you understand? Right, well, here goes. I've eliminated all the conventional ones. Maybe it's metafiction. Or a genre mash-up . . .'

Bradley began to growl threateningly.

'. . . We could be in a science fiction novel,' explained Sam, 'for all I know.'

'That would be fun,' said Horace.

'Shut up or I'll smash your face in,' said Bradley.

Horace looked at Sam and saw a trickle of blood coming from his hairline, following his recent beating. He shut up.

After another glowering look at Sam, Bradley got out of the car and came round to his door. 'Here we go again,' said Sam, hoping that if he got another bash to the head at least it would knock him out. Bradley ejected him from the vehicle and pointed up at the sky.

'A science fiction novel,' he said. 'So you're saying a flying saucer would appear right now?'

'Not a flying saucer,' said Sam. 'No one believes in flying saucers these days. More like some sort of heavily armoured spacecraft, or perhaps an enormous mother ship. Like that one . . .'

Bradley let go of Sam, sending the writer crashing to the floor again as he, and all the people in the square, looked up and saw a huge dark shape fill the sky.

Chapter Nineteen

ABOVE THEM in the sky was something that at first glance looked to the detective (who lacked any other frame of reference) like a mile-long carburettor. Its main difference in appearance from this common piece of machinery was in the circular orange lights that glowed from its sides, and perhaps in the thousand smaller white specks glimmering from its millions of windows. Spiky, hundred-yard-long antennae extended from the front, and the whole structure was a sequence of giant spheres, hexagons and cuboid structures attached to each other by triangulated scaffolds through which ran spiralling supply pipes and walkways as wide as roads. The surface was of some dark, hard matt substance that hardly reflected light but gleamed meagrely, and the impression it struck on all the humans who gazed up at it was one of stupefied horror and awe. All voices fell silent; the helicopters scooted away across the trees to safety. The soldiers pointed their rifles upwards, useless as ants staring up at a tree about to fall.

There came one giant, glaring note from an instrument

within the spacecraft like an intergalactic foghorn, a frightening blast that blew out all the windows and sent a gust through the square, leaving all the humans clutching their ears. Then a narrow spindly shaft of glittering light flickered down and widened to a spotlight upon the cobblestones.

'BEHOLD!' thundered a voice. 'The one and only Zaltor the Merciless!'

There was a blinding flash and suddenly there in front of them, standing in the spotlight, was a strange creature in a white space suit. It seemed humanoid, with pale skin and wild red curly hair that sprouted from the back of its head in a sort of ginger halo. Behind it stood another figure with a notepad.

'Behold,' said the creature, coughing politely, and reading from a flimsy piece of foolscap he held in front of him. 'For I am Zaltor the Merciless, Lord of the Seven Moons. I am here to demand from you, citizens of Naxi-Mori-Dolli-Phumofillimoltimollibosss (often referred to as Percy for short), that you deliver unto us the Gem-laden Sword of Shlorb. Or we'll be really cross. And when I say really cross, I mean *really* cross.' Finishing what was on the sheet, he looked up and coughed modestly. 'It's a bit on the nose as pronouncements go, but there you are, name of the game, really. Er . . . Why are you all looking at me like that?'

Sam looked around him. Everyone else seemed speechless with terror and/or in the process of having a stroke.

'Er . . .' he piped up timidly. 'We're not actually the, er, the citizens of . . . Where did you say?'

'The risk with talking to aliens,' Sam thought, 'is that you really don't know how they're going to react.' He half expected to be zapped into a small pile of ash, but instead Zaltor blinked three times and said: 'Naxi-Mori-Phumos. Did I say it right?'

'Not if you meant to say "Earth". This is Earth.'

Zaltor waited a beat, then turned round and said to his underling, 'Earth? We're on fucking *Earth*? We're not even in the right galaxy, Chris. Are you kidding me?'

'Maybe I got the coordinates wrong,' said the second alien, looking at his notepad.

'Yeah, I'm guessing you fucking did get the coordinates wrong, you dungwit! That's right, I said "dungwit"! And I'm not taking it back. *Earth*!' He spat the last word in disgust, as they both looked up into the spotlight and twiddled buttons on their watches.

'Oh, er, sorry about that,' said Zaltor the Merciless. 'Do carry on. Is this a party? Well, have a good time.'

Then he zapped back into space with a scarcely audible blip.

Everyone looked around, dazed, at one another for a moment before the yellow glittering spotlight shone back down again on exactly the same spot. Zaltor once more flickered into being in front of them.

'Wait a minute . . . Earth,' he said. 'You created Spaghetti Carbonara, right?'

'Er, yes,' said Sam.

'And cricket? And the cryptic crossword?'

'That too.'

'Cracking!' said Zaltor. 'Keep up the good work, and see you in a thousand years. Toodle-pip!'

There was another flash of light, Zaltor disappeared again, there came another deafening blast from the foghorn and the spaceship blinked out of the sky.

Bradley looked at Sam. 'Metafiction, you say?'

Sam shrugged, then looked around. 'What's that sound?' he asked.

'It's the ship,' said Bradley, 'flying off.'

'I don't think it is,' said Sam, concerned. 'It seemed to just blip off to another galaxy. Can you hear that rumbling?'

'I can't hear anything,' said Bradley.

'I think it's coming from the Hill. Hey, look! That didn't used to be there.'

Sam pointed to one corner of the square. 'Wasn't that where Yeay Thee Olde Curiosity Tea Shoppe used to be? Now there's just a huge towering pile of rubbish!'

But Bradley wasn't listening. Sam's mention of the Hill had brought to his attention the one avenue to do with Fairbreath's disappearance that they hadn't had an answer to. He marched over to where the townspeople were being guarded at gunpoint. The members of the Parish Council had huddled together, as though they were having an ad hoc meeting. The mayor saw Bradley coming and piped up.

'Oh it's you, Bradley, you utterly brainless bumhole! What is the bloody meaning of arresting my butler in the middle of the night?'

'Shut it, fatso, or I'll knock your teeth out!'

The mayor then saw Sam and recalled what had happened to him shortly before the interruption of Zaltor the Merciless. He shut up.

'Why was Terry Fairbreath interested in the Hill? What is it that you're trying to keep secret about it?'

They all looked at each other nervously. None of them wanted to be the first to speak.

'The Hill?' piped up Horace, who had come over to watch. 'You should have asked me. It's full of shit.'

Bradley elbowed him in the stomach so forcefully he doubled up and collapsed over, clutching his belly with his handcuffed hands. 'No, I mean it, it's literally full of rubbish,' he said from the ground.

'God damn it, be quiet, Horace!' shouted Lord Selvington. 'Or I'll jolly well cut off your allowance!'

'Whoop de doo,' said Horace.

'Go on,' said Bradley. 'Tell us about the Hill?'

'Well, after the Second World War the town was impoverished, and there was this landfill site a few miles away. We were offered a lot of money to have it put here. The town used the money to start doing itself up, becoming a picture-perfect tourist trap.'

'So where did the rubbish go?'

'Under the Hill. Twenty million tonnes of it. They just turfed it over and pretended it wasn't there. If anyone found out then the town would lose its reputation.'

'Is it just me,' said Sam, pointing to the same corner of the square as before, 'or is that pile substantially *bigger* than it was a few moments ago?' But no one was listening to him.

'Terry started hearing about the old murders that had happened, got interested and they bumped him off.'

'*No!*' shouted Selvington. 'It's not true! He was poking around, yes – but there's nothing to find. I swear it. Those murders were solved and the perpetrators caught.'

'Shut it, you toilet!' shouted Bradley.

'Er, guys . . .' said Sam.

'I'm arresting you all on suspicion of murder. On SUS-PICION . . . of . . .' Bradley was finding it hard to be heard beneath a background roaring noise. 'Of . . . MURDER!'

'GUYS!' shouted Sam, grabbing Bradley's sleeve. 'We've got to go!' He pointed at the pile of rubbish in the corner, which was now not only substantially more massive than before, but visibly growing. 'I think the noise of the space-ship must have affected it. It's bursting!'

'Shit!' said Bradley.

'Literally,' said Horace. 'I've always wanted to say that.'

The rubbish spilled out onto the square now like rapid lava from a nearby volcano, falling in cascading waves in the centre and oozing around the edges.

'Well, I've always wanted to say this,' said Sam. 'Let's get the hell out of here!'

'Okay, let's go!' Bradley shouted to the soldiers, and their commanding officer waved them away to the south corner of the square, the townspeople running with them. As they all ran, however, the road collapsed in front of them and a poisonous gust of rancid air spilled out in a dark cloud. Many screamed and fell back. The major, taking his eyepatch off, yodelled at the sky, having apparently now gone mad for real. The soldiers shouted urgently into their walkie-talkies as another terrible rumble and roar came down from the mountainside. A massive sprouting stream of garbage spewed out from a fresh hole, high as a tsunami, and engulfed the street leading from the north of the square.

The helicopters came thumping across the rooftops and hovered above them.

'Hurry!' shouted Bradley and Sam, and the soldiers waved their arms furiously. Rope ladders were dropped from six different aircraft, and with agonizing slowness the old people started to climb, encouraged with shouts from the soldiers.

The noises, infernal burpings and explosions continued to come. The abbey was shattered into a pile of stones, and the houses on the north side of the square were sucked down from inside and crumpled, falling inwards and disappearing completely.

'I'm not satisfied,' shouted Bradley into Sam's ear. 'we've not solved the case!'

'Okay, but can we talk about it later?' Sam shouted back. Then a thought struck him. 'Oh my God!' he shouted. 'What about the children at the school?'

The pair exchanged a terrified look before Bradley's expression cleared and he pointed into the sky. There, buzzing between the helicopters and darting in and around the tops of the roofs, were a hundred or so children, flying on broomsticks.

There was so much to take in at once that Sam didn't have time to question what this meant – and now it was his and Bradley's turn to jump on the rope. The soldiers had mounted onto other craft that rose ahead of them and as his foot left the cobblestones the detective felt them tremble beneath him. When he had a firm grip he looked down and saw the stones all shaking and chattering, before the pattern dissolved and only churning mud was left. A fast-moving pool of slurry spread across the surface of the square, as fast as a breaking wave, a hellish odour rising from it.

The helicopter lifted up, just as the few remaining walls of houses were flooded, and shattered on the impact, or a second later were overcome with trash. As the chopper rose, banked and sped towards distant safety, the last traces of the town disappeared under the tidal wave of shit.

Chapter Twenty

THE SMALL FLEET of helicopters (and broomsticks) hugged the treeline as it crossed miles of clear countryside touched only by early-morning sunshine. For a moment all the children were out of sight and as he gazed into the rising sun, it felt to Sam like this madness was all imagined, and he wondered whether this would make for the television pilot he had always wanted to write.

'No,' he thought, 'the budget would be way too high.' He looked at Bradley, and realized that for him the case was really still unresolved. 'I forgot to tell him about the other kind of detective novel,' he reflected, 'the kind where the case remains unsolved and sticks in the detective's mind for years on end, becoming an obsession with him. Oh, well.'

They were set down at an army base some twenty miles south that had been put on emergency. Ambulances were there, ready for those suffering from injuries, panic and (in seven instances) mild heart attacks. There was one sight which had haunted them all as they had risen into the sky from the doomed town and that was the cordoned area in the east end of the square, where Bradley had put the granny mafia under armed watch. This had become cut off at the last minute and none of the grannies had survived.

'Good,' said Bradley. 'Serves the fuckwits right.'

The survivors were given blankets and taken into the mess hall, where hot drinks and soup were offered them in cups. After several dozen loud complaints, the soup and tea were replaced by 'medicinal' brandy from the store, which was ladled out into tin cups and some time after that, the ancient crowd was subdued into sad and quiet conversations, or sleep.

Bradley was not for hanging around, though. There was something on his mind and without delay he seconded a jeep from the army base (which came with a soldier in it, to check he didn't put it to misuse) and headed back to Fraxbridge as fast as he could. Sam saw him turning on the motor and jumped in the back at the last minute.

'Wait for me!' he said. 'I want to come.'

'Okay,' said Bradley, speeding out of the gate. 'But there's no time. Something's about to go down, I can feel it.'

They hit a bridge and lifted off for twenty yards, landing with a tremendous smash. The soldier's rifle went off.

'Whoopsadaisy,' he said.

'There's something else, Sam,' said Bradley. 'Something

you haven't told me; something you've forgotten. I can feel it. You said I ignore the evidence, right?'

'Right. Follow your gut.'

'But you mean the *legal* evidence, right? The stuff my superintendent would care about.'

'Yes, I suppose you're right. You should pay attention to the little stuff, the little signs of wrongdoing that aren't exactly evidence, but *clues*.'

'*Exactly*,' Bradley repeated, as they tore round a corner. 'There's something. Something someone said; something troubling the back of my mind.'

'But we've left behind all the suspects at the military base,' protested Sam.

'The *obvious* suspects,' said Bradley. 'The butlers, all the other residents . . . Something doesn't fit.'

They raced down a country lane at approaching three times what Sam would have regarded as a safe speed. His training of Bradley had nearly come to fruition: he was sharing a car with the detective of his dreams, and now he wasn't entirely sure he wanted to. But he was proud of his creation – not to give encouragement now would be like Frankenstein taking a hammer to the monster just as it raised its head.

'You're right, Detective. You've got all the pieces, you just need to put them together. The chances are you'll puzzle over it and then at the last minute you will be put

onto the scent by an apparently innocuous remark by someone else – possibly one that, when you think back over it,
comes across as rather shoehorned in. By the way, that last
line you said about how something doesn't fit – that's perfect. You're becoming a natural.'

'Well, something *doesn't* fit. What is it that's troubling
me? Tell me all the events in the last twenty-four hours.' He
was nearly hitting ninety now, the trees that lined the lane
racing past, the light flitting through. The soldier sat quite
happily next to him, unperturbed.

'The pub. The landlord . . .'

'Braindead.'

'The grannies . . .'

'Actually dead.'

'The car, the field, the golf clubs, the ogre . . .'

'Almost certainly dead.'

'The driver who picked us up.'

'Again – braindead.'

Sam thought there was something exciting and fearful
about Bradley's intensity. He himself had been perfectly certain there was no crime to solve, but the detective's ferocity
was starting to make him feel otherwise and causing an
uncomfortable cold sensation to rise through him. They
tore through a small hamlet that was still asleep, ripped
straight over the roundabout in the middle of the road, took
a left turning too late and missed the bridge – instead they

hit an abandoned truckbed that leant to the ground and formed an improvised ramp, and, hitting it at nearly a hundred, they cleared the stream easily, landing with a resounding crash that made the soldier's rifle go off again.

'Whoopsadaisy,' he said once more.

Bradley angled the jeep through a farm's back yard, avoiding several chickens before smashing through a bush and hitting the road again. He looked at his watch.

'Fried chicken,' said Sam.

'Delicious.'

'Horace, the Duke of Rochester.'

'Daft,' said Bradley.

'The butlers . . .'

'Innocent.'

'The square. The soldiers . . .'

'There *is something*,' insisted Bradley.

'The spaceship.' Sam tried to think laterally. 'The Tea Shoppe. The cobbles. The drugs . . .'

'Ooh, have you got any drugs?' asked the soldier.

'*No!*' they both said.

'The car, the full moon, the rubbish . . . I can feel it, I'm close . . .'

The engine started smoking as Bradley reached the edge of Fraxbridge and began emitting flames by the time they hit the high street. He slew to a halt by the side of the street and left it where it stopped, then got out and ran.

'Slow down!' shouted Sam. 'I'm injured, for God's sake. By you!'

'Hurry,' said Bradley, slowing to a jog.

'What's going on?'

'I don't know but I have to get back to the police station. Yes,' he went on quietly. 'It all ties in together. The spaceship had nothing to do with it. A ticking time bomb . . .'

'That bomb was part of all this?' Sam hobbled along as the soldier jogged happily beside him.

'You can't carry me, can you?' he asked.

'Nope,' said the soldier.

'Yes. It all fits together, but I can't work out how. The rubbish had already started to appear. You remember the pile outside the library when we got there?'

'Yes, of course,' said Sam, surprised.

'Well, you know how all those explosions keep coming from within the grounds of the school and no one seems to think anything's up? Like when my car exploded. No one took any notice, or came looking. They're used to explosions. So a bomb was laid somewhere near the base of the Hill. The whole thing was triggered deliberately, ahead of time.'

He came to a stop, and they stood in front of the blown-out police station offices. Sam bent over, wheezing, begging for them not to go on again for a moment. Straightening, he plucked the bottle of rum out of his inner pocket and had begun to swig when it was snatched by Bradley, who drank it like Lawrence of Arabia helping himself to his waterskin. Looking on askance, Sam instead lit a cigarette and immediately doubled up again, his throat rent by a horrible tearing cough.

'When this is over I've got to sort out my act,' he said. 'I'm too old for this shit.' He held the cigarette away and took a breath of clean air, coughed again and whimpered somewhat. 'I sound like a werewolf.'

Bradley took the bottle from his mouth and tossed it aside – Sam was lucky to catch it, and got a splash across his shirt for his efforts.

'Werewolf . . .' said Bradley, looking up at the morning sky. Sam and the soldier followed his gaze. With the sun still low near the horizon, it was a beautiful, clear pale blue, with nothing in it except the half moon, clearly visible.

'You know what I feel?' Bradley said to Sam.

'No, what?'

'The hairs on the back of my neck are standing on end. For real. Werewolf! That's it!' he said, and pointed to the soldier. '*You*, come here!'

UPSTAIRS IN THE first-floor squad room, as Sam called it, all was quiet. It made for a desperately sad sight. The walls were scorched black, desks charred and chairs turned over.

There were standing pools of water from the fire-engine hoses that had soaked the building to ensure the fire had gone out. There were flame patterns across the ceiling, interspersed with sections where the paint had mottled and melted, and where the plaster sagged in damp bulges, ready to collapse. Where the windows had been, remnants of the plastic blinds hung and moved gently in the breeze so that the early-morning sun slanted inwards, making a slow-motion strobing effect.

A tall figure came in slowly through the door, treading with great caution. He squinted through the dimness, trying to make out a shape amid the mingling of the sunlight with the ashen air and last traces of smoke.

Soon he saw what he expected in the centre of the room and stood stock still. But it was too late – he had been spotted. A crouching figure was feeling through the soggy embers and half-burned papers around Detective Brautigan's desk, whispering to itself incessantly. But now it stopped and turned its head to the door.

The tattered blinds shifted in the wind and light fell across the face.

'Terry Fairbreath,' said the tall figure, its face still in darkness.

'*You,*' whispered the crouching man. 'You, of all people! The idiot detective! You were supposed to be dead.'

'I know,' said the tall figure. 'You planned it all. You

uncovered the secret of the Hill, and planted a bomb to explode it and destroy the town. But first you wanted to fake your own death so that it was recorded before the evidence was destroyed.'

'Yes,' uttered Fairbreath, hate narrowing his voice to a whisper. 'I planned it perfectly. It took months! That reliably snooping old battleaxe Mrs Bottlescum was supposed to see me being convincingly massacred. How could I know the stupid old cow had the attention span of a gnat? The second I was out of sight, covered in fake blood, she just forgot the whole damn thing!'

'That was your first mistake,' said the figure.

'Oh, don't patronize me. You got lucky! It's that bloody writer who's been following you around, filling your head with ideas,' said Terry Fairbreath scornfully. 'I suppose he's with you now.'

'No, actually – he's succumbed to his many injuries. And rum. He fell asleep outside.'

'You know what I came here for?'

'The one piece of evidence you left behind at the scene of one of the murders. You knew Brautigan had it, that it linked you to the prostitute murders in Fraxbridge. And you had to find a way to get in here and retrieve it.'

'How did you solve all this?'

'Just a hunch,' said the tall figure. 'About the Full Moon Murderer. The major told us you went away once a month to visit your mother and I guessed that was exactly when these killings were going on. You disappeared on the day of the full moon, when you committed your last murder. But the body was only found and the case handed on to Brautigan last night. It took me too long to put two and two together . . .'

'And make five?'

'Well . . . no. Four, surely?'

'It's a saying,' said Fairbreath.

'Right. But it doesn't really work in this con— Well, let's not quibble over that right now. After what happened to Mumford, the bomb going off here was too much of a coincidence. I decided you were coming back here to reclaim some evidence.'

'I can't believe it,' said Fairbreath. '*You*! You never entered my calculations. You were nothing – just another casualty. A vacant casualty. Now you're going to arrest me, I suppose?'

'I was considering it,' said the tall figure out of the corner of its mouth.

Fairbreath bent over, looking distraught, cradling his head. Then one of his hands shot down into the water at his feet and came back up, holding the semi-automatic handgun in the evidence bag that had been hanging on the edge of Brautigan's desk.

'Fucking Brautigan!' said the tall figure. 'What is it with

him and not doing paperwork? So there's something to be said for filing things properly after all – Bradley was right!'

'Bradley?' repeated Fairbreath uncertainly.

'Too right,' said a voice from a dark corner at the other end of the room. 'You put that gun down or I'm going to punch your stupid face into mashed potato, you toilet! And that's not just hyperbollocks . . .'

Fairbreath spun round, pulling the trigger, as startled as anyone else when the gun fired a stuttering burst, emptying half its clip into spattering explosions against the far wall, all the bullets save for one, which hit the detective in the chest. A nasty jet of dark substance jumped from his chest in the gloom and he fell over on his back.

Fairbreath didn't wait to see if he had killed him. He had clearly studied the building well and instead of running for the door blocked by Sam in Bradley's coat, he turned towards the fire escape, gun in hand.

A much louder noise boomed through the room, the sound not of a handgun, but an army-issue rifle. Fairbreath's whole body was tilted towards the fire escape door as he saw it open and caught a glimpse of the firearm facing him. But the strength of the shot picked him up, spun him over in mid-air and finally dissipated, letting him splash into a dark puddle six feet behind.

'Whoopsadaisy,' said the soldier.

Epilogue

DETECTIVE INSPECTOR Bradley was aware of a great deal of pain pretty much all the time. It only quietened down when he could manage sleep, and for a while after the nurse visited to change his morphine drip. Mostly he was kept awake, immobile and in a kind of quiet agony. And pissed off.

He spent most of the first two days drugged beyond consciousness, but at lunchtime on the third day he woke to see Sam reading a Raymond Chandler novel in a chair nearby.

'What do you want?' he asked.

'That's the detective I know!' said Sam happily, putting down his book. 'How are you feeling?'

'How would you feel if you had a lung with a bullet hole in it?'

Sam thought about this for a moment.

'Like shit,' he said. 'But in need of a drink.'

Bradley grunted, not wanting to move, but trying to spot what Sam held in his other hand until he lifted it up so the detective could see. It was a bottle of ginger ale.

'Oh great,' said Bradley. 'You *are* a fucking help.'

'Hey!' said Sam, outraged. 'What am I, a damn rookie? Would I bring you bloody grapes and a copy of *Grazia*? There's a slosh of ginger ale in there and no more. You know what the rest is. Or you will, soon after you have a slug. And here,' Sam leant in conspiratorially. 'Let's get *Stalag 17* about this. I'm not smuggling this in just for it to be confiscated. Here's what you do. I don't want the nurses doling out your ginger ale in case they catch a whiff of it, so I'm hiding it under your bag in your locker here, and here's a little hip flask for your pillow – it's full. Get trusted guests to pour it out for you, okay?' He illustrated this point by slurping a fair measure into two paper cups and handing one to his friend.

Bradley looked into his cup and sniffed the liquid. 'I've never said this to someone younger than me before,' he said, 'but you're probably going to die young.'

'Up yours,' said Sam, toasting him and taking a sip.

'Cheers,' grumbled Bradley, wincing at the pain of holding it up with the arm from his good side. 'How are the townspeople, are they okay?'

'Yes, I think so. Except for the vicar. It turns out that Mrs Trench was Terry Fairbreath all along, that's how he knew what was going on.'

'Bloody hell, no wonder he's so surprised,' Bradley said, taken aback.

'That's not the half of it. He'd been letting her suck him off for the past three months. Cheers to you, you old stinker!' said Sam.

'You've been *drinking*, you slag!' Bradley said sharply.

'Well, I couldn't fit all the whisky in the ginger ale bottle, could I? What would you want me to do, throw it down the drain?'

Bradley grunted. 'Open the curtains, would you?'

'A pleasure. Your wife been round?'

'Three times. You can't make them keep her out of here, can you?'

'I don't think I can. And think of her feelings, old man – she cares for you.'

Bradley grunted yet again.

'She didn't realize what an absolute dishpot she'd married,' Sam went on.

'Okay, that's enough. Give me another slug of that stuff and clear off. I can't handle *two* pains at once!'

Sam raised his eyebrows, did the service he was asked and shuffled to the door.

'Hey,' said Bradley, his bluff called. Sam turned round.

'Why didn't you help me crack it sooner?'

'I didn't realize we were doing a *serial killer* thriller. All the signs pointed the other way. How could I have guessed?'

'We going to do another case together?'

'I don't think so. As your civilian sidekick, I think the

routine is that I would normally clear off at the end and next time you'd get another sidekick.'

'Well,' said Bradley, clearly having some trouble with how to phrase the next sentence. 'You were pretty useful,' he admitted grudgingly. 'Pretty annoying, but pretty useful.'

'Nice of you to say so.'

'That's all you get. Oh – and thanks for the whisky.'

'Any time, man. See you later.'

Sam paused at the door and winked at Bradley, then left. A minute later he put his head back round the door.

'Wanted to say – I don't really care about these things, but for your own sake, next car you get, don't make it a Prius.'

'Wasn't my intention to,' said Bradley. 'But thanks for your input. Any other suggestions, stick 'em on a postcard!'

Sam disappeared once more.

Bradley let his mind wander for a while, hoping to persuade the pain away or in some way out-think it, and must have fallen into a light doze because he was suddenly awoken by a huge shape at the end of his bed. He was by no means yet over the shock of having been shot and the sight made him start – which provoked a nauseating wave of pain. He screwed up his face as he waited for it to pass and the man standing there came to the side of his bed.

'Didn't mean to surprise you,' he said shortly.

'That's okay. Pain's something I've got to live with now.'

'I understand,' said Brautigan, and there was no doubt that he did. There was a huge gauze over his right cheek, stitches along his jaw, a nasty black bruise above his right eye and his left arm was so firmly encased in plaster that it had been fixed to his waist with a splint so that it stuck out immovably.

'It should have been me,' said Brautigan in that deep voice, which was so rumbling it sounded like a heavy table being moved in the next room.

Bradley shrugged. 'I got lucky.'

The other detective laughed. 'I guess I was lucky to only be blown up!'

'Listen,' said Bradley. 'I hope you don't think I was stepping on your toes. I always wanted to crack cases like you.'

'But you cracked the biggest one of all. I got to admit, I never thought you were a real dick, and now I know you were.'

Bradley couldn't meet his eye. 'If you like,' he said, 'you solve one for me some time.'

Brautigan put his hand, which was roughly the size and weight of a skillet, on Bradley's shoulder and squeezed in what he might have thought was a friendly way, but which in reality would probably have snapped an elephant's leg. It was all Bradley could do not to pass out from the pain.

'Let's get a hamburger some time,' said Brautigan, and arranging the muscles and pulverized cartilage of his face into a curious arrangement that was even more grotesque than usual, he went out, banging the plaster-cast of his left arm against the side of the door as he went and swearing loudly. He was smiling, thought Bradley.

Bradley's gaze wandered to the window and he grumpily surveyed the view – a huge swathe of sky, bright and yellow in the afternoon sun, interrupted only by the rectangular block of another part of the hospital and a tall chimney in which Bradley had his suspicions they burned amputated body parts. He shivered.

'Not even a bloody telly!' he said, looking over at his bedside table and wincing from the movement. He hadn't noticed before, but something had been left there for him, and he knew who by. Standing almost a foot tall, there was a pile of paperbacks, some announcing their titles in garish colours and fonts, others older and plainer. He leant over and picked one up – on the back it described itself as a classic of the crime genre. He leafed to the front and started to look through it, wondering whether this was where he would find out who his next sidekick would be.